12.00

Road Race

BY THE AUTHOR

Road Race
Southpaw from San Francisco
Blackburn's Headhunters
Young Skin Diver
Game, Carol Canning!
Breakaway Back

ROAD RACE

By PHILIP HARKINS

Thomas Y. Crowell Company
NEW YORK

Acknowledgments

This book could not have been written without a great deal of technical help from two experts, A. J. Hoe and Gayle Smith.

Jim Hoe, owner of Hoe Sportcar, Westport, Connecticut, has raced his own Duesenberg at Bridgehampton and Watkins Glen. Gayle Smith, now of the United States Army, has won drag races against MGs with the Model A he built in his own backyard in Weston, Connecticut.

Writing this book was, for the author, like learning how to drive. And as this book was driven by its student-driver, experts Hoe and Smith followed it patiently, figuratively fixing flats, cleaning carburetors, and keeping it headed in the right direction.

Also helping along the way were two other technical advisers to whom thanks must be given, Hagen Morris of Westport and W. T. Sperry of Danbury, Connecticut.

Road Race

Chapter I

THE hill was so steep Dave had to get off his bike and walk on the tar road still wet from a thunder shower. Sweat ran down his face, blurring his eyes, tickling his nose, and leaving a salty taste on his lips. The bike seemed to fight him, as if it knew it was outgrown and that the burden it was forced to carry held the means to its unhappy end. For the burden was a battery and spark plugs with which Dave hoped to start his hot rod.

Reaching the top of the hill Dave stopped to catch his breath, then pedaled on past a sign that said BRANCHVILLE. Beyond it the road dipped sharply; and the bike, changing its tactics, eagerly rushed downhill as if to show its owner how fast it would go. Wind

1

whooshed by Dave's ears and cooled his perspiring face. But it was a refreshing rather than an exhilarating ride. When Dave thought of speed these days he thought of a hot rod, not a bicycle.

Coasting past Chet Coley's filling station Dave braked, skidding a little on the slippery road, took a right turn, and pedaled hard down the straight flat stretch that marked the entrance to the Codman farm. Then he saw it, standing by the chicken coop, and his heart lifted. How could his mother have possibly called it "a hunk of junk"? Why it was a wonderful Model A, a 1930 four-cylinder Ford—a magnificent gift from Farmer Codman. Oh sure, it was rusty, scarred, dented; it needed all kinds of replacements for worn-out parts; it even needed a new frame. But most of all it needed a great deal of work and that was what Dave was willing and anxious to supply.

Quickly leaning his bike against a convenient tree Dave hurried away with spark plugs and battery. *Crash*. The bike fell to the ground. Impatient, annoyed, Dave hurried on. Then on a sudden impulse he stopped, turned back, put down his burden, picked up the bike and leaned it carefully against the tree. A faithful machine that had provided adequate transportation should not be carelessly abandoned just because it had been outgrown.

About half an hour later Dave entered a shack which he used as an auxiliary toolshop and, emerging

2

with a two-gallon can of gasoline, carefully emptied it in the Model A's fuel tank. Then, like a scientist anxiously awaiting the outcome of a great experiment, he stepped on the starter.

Arruruh—ruruh—ruruh. Silence. *Arruruh—ruruh—ruruh.* No answer. *Arruruh—ruh—carrumph—rumph—carmph.* It caught; it roared; it squawked like a new-born baby greeting the world. And Dave listened like a proud obstetrician. What a glorious noise—how brash, how confident. But what was that? Dave's ears cocked at a suspicious cough. He frowned as the cough became a rasp, a gasp, a sputter. And, though Dr. Dave gave frantic first aid, the patient passed out.

Undismayed, Dave got the Model A going again and started probing for the cause of the failure. It might be the spark plugs, might be the carburetor. What about that water trap, the small glass bowl a couple of feet above the exhaust pipe? What was in the bowl, water or gas? Normally, Dave knew, there would be gas in the bowl. Any water swirling in would sink to the bottom being heavier than gas, and be trapped. But was it working that way?

The engine answered Dave's question by again sputtering to a stop. It must be the water trap. Dave reached over, eagerly undid the screw, grasped the glass bowl in his greasy fingers. It slipped. *Crash.* It landed on the exhaust pipe and broke. *Whoom*—it exploded. *Fire!*

3

Dave scrambled for safety, horrified by his slip and its calamitous result. But even as the flames shot skyward his mechanically minded brain analyzed the accident. It was gas in the trap, not water, and it had been ignited by the heat of the exhaust pipe.

Fire! Fire! A terrible exclamation on a farm. And Farmer Codman dashed up with a bucket of water.

Dave stepped in front of the farmer. "Don't throw water on it!"

"Ye outter yer mind, young feller?" Farmer Codman sweating, panting, was poised like a minute man but with bucket instead of gun. "Git outter my way!"

Dave stood his ground. "Don't, Mr. Codman! Water spreads a gasoline fire."

"Dern you Dave and your hifalutin' ideas! D'y' want my chicken coop burnt t' the ground? Now get outter my way or I'll—"

Splash. Refusing to budge Dave had taken the full contents of the bucket on face and chest. The sudden shower shocked him into action. He seized the bucket from Mr. Codman and scooped up some fine dirt from a convenient pile, throwing it on the flames to extinguish the fire.

"Waal I'll be dol gurned." Mr. Codman tipped back his straw hat and scratched his bald head. "Durned if you weren't right, Dave—dirt did put out the fire. And I'm sorry I got ye so wet, young feller." Mr. Codman cackled. "But it was only water and you were probably overheated anyway."

"Yeah." Dave smiled ruefully. "Guess I was."

Mr. Codman wagged his head, clucked his tongue. "Can't have fires and explosions around here, young feller, scares the dickens out of my chickens. Look at 'em. Some of 'em have run clear across the road. We'd better—hey there—watch out for that chicken!"

There was a car coming down the road, a jalopy. Its driver suddenly saw the flapping, squawking chicken. The driver braked, the jalopy swerved and with a plaintive sob from its tires skidded off the road. *Crash.* It rammed into the tall, thick elm.

The elm resisted, the jalopy succumbed, and Mr. Codman, pushing back his straw hat, said, "Dol gurn that reckless driver. He not only durned near killed one of my chickens but he damaged the only healthy elum left in the township."

Dave's reactions were different. "Come on!" he cried, running toward the wreck. As he ran he had sickening visions of spattered blood, torn flesh, broken bones. He felt like running the other way but he forced himself in the direction of the smash-up.

There was no spattered blood, no torn flesh. The driver was simply scared and hemmed in by crumpled metal. Dave got the door open and helped the victim out on the road.

He was quite a victim, a short roly-poly man with a

5

double chin and a mustache waxed to two sharp points. His clothes and his complexion reminded Dave of one of those dazzling combinations of ice cream, fruit, and sauce that grace the soda fountains of the nation, namely a banana split. The stranger's shirt had the soft creamy color of a banana. His necktie and matching hatband suggested a slab of strawberry, vanilla, and chocolate ice cream with just a touch of pistachio. His round, soft face represented the marshmallow in the mess and his sunburned forehead was the cherry that tops the gooey conglomeration.

Dave's anxiety struggled through his fascination and he asked, "You all right mister?"

A chubby hand decorated with a huge black and gold signet ring reached for the mustache and though trembling, deftly twisted one of the waxed points. A deep and vibrant voice boomed from a cherubic mouth, "The Yankees will win again," it said.

"Huh?" said Dave. He feared that the man had a case of brain concussion.

Stubby fingers twirled another waxed point. "A stupid question deserves a stupid answer. Obviously I am all right, son. I have walked away from worse wrecks than this at The Bridge and The Glen."

Dave's mouth was still open in astonishment but words stumbled out of it. "The bridge? The glen?"

"Bridgehampton, Watkins Glen." The booming voice turned condescending. "Road races, son."

6

"You drive in road races?" gasped Dave. "In that heap?" Dave nodded at the wreckage the stranger had left behind him. The jalopy's radiator had crumbled, the engine had disappeared, the top had collapsed; it looked like a total loss.

The stranger contemptuously surveyed the shambles, disdainfully dismissed them with a wave of a hand. "That corpse? Of corpse not." The stranger chuckled. "Get it? Not a bad pun, ay? Might work it into one of my scripts."

Scripts? Bridgehampton? Watkins Glen? Dave was completely confused.

The stranger drew forth a long, thin, pigskin wallet, flipped it open, produced a card. Dave took it numbly, held it gingerly with greasy fingers, read it with widening eyes. It was a curious card. In the center, big bright red letters against a blue background spelled out NEGLEY FOXCROFT. Underneath the name white letters said "Television Actor." And the third line down, again in red letters said, "Member of the Sports Car Club of America."

Negley Foxcroft was twirling the points of his mustache. His voice was deeper, more vibrant than ever. "You have undoubtedly seen me on TV, young man?"

Still staring at the card Dave shook his head, "We don't have a set," he said.

"You *what*?" The points of the waxed mustache

7

shot skyward in astonishment. The marshmallow face shook, the sunburned forehead turned a riper red. "No TV set in this day and age? How incredible, how backward—how come?"

Dave shrugged his shoulders. "Just couldn't afford one, I guess. Ma's still makin' payments on the washing machine."

"Why my dear young man." Negley Foxcroft's vibrant voice proceeded to deliver a short lecture on the wonders of TV. But Dave wasn't listening. He was again reading the red, white, and blue card, particularly the third line, Sports Car ˙Club of America. Could that be some kind of hot rod club? He asked the question of Negley Foxcroft who had paused for breath.

"Hot rod club?" The waxed points of the mustache shot up again. "Good heavens no! The Sports Car Club is a dignified and conservative organization dedicated to the grace, nobility, and speed of the sports car."

"Oh," said Dave. He rubbed the back of his hand against his chin and nodded his head toward the remains of the jalopy. "Then this really wasn't a heap?"

"A heap? Please speak English, young man."

"A rod. A souped up job."

"Oh goodness no!" Negley Foxcroft shook with haughty amusement. "That was just a jalopy I used to take me to the railroad station. Picked it up for fifty or a hundred bucks. I'll junk it and get another. Or maybe I'll get an MG. I really need a better second car. I don't like to use my XK; besides Webb Walden is tuning it up for the Glen."

Dave scratched his head. Why couldn't Negley Foxcroft use terms a guy could understand like "heap" and "hot rod?" A road race at the Glen had become comprehensible but MG and XK were mysterious and who was Webb Walden—some master mechanic?

Dave was trying to sort out all these strange new facts when a nasal voice twanged into the confusing conversation. Mr. Codman, having first taken care of his own property, making sure that the fire was out and all the chickens safely off the road, had now come up to deliver his opinion of the smash-up.

"Too bad about that elum," he said, "ain't many good elums left in the state."

Negley Foxcroft's mustache bristled. "Are you by any chance drawing an invidious comparison between the preservation of an elm and the safety of my sponsor's best salesman?"

Mr. Codman gawked. "What are you talkin' about?"

Dave tried to explain. He had been critically examining the wreck to see if something could be salvaged. His interest was aroused by what he found. The wreck had been a Model A. The engine was a mess but the frame seemed intact. And a Model A frame was just what Dave needed. Now if only Mr. Foxcroft proved reasonable.

"Mr. Foxcroft is a famous TV actor," said Dave diplomatically, hoping that Mr. Foxcroft would be pleased by the introduction.

He was. But Mr. Codman was not impressed. "Never heard of him," he said laconically and, though the waxed mustache twitched indignantly, Mr. Codman twanged right ahead. "And you had no right running into that elum, Mr. Boxtop—it's one of the last healthy elums in the state."

"Healthy elms!" cried Negley Foxcroft. "How about *my* health? I'm lucky to be alive for the future benefit of my vast TV audience. And all on account of your idiotic chicken. I've a good mind to sue you for creating a traffic hazard."

"If ye do," cried Mr. Codman, "I'll sue you right back for damagin' that elum!"

"Preposterous!" cried Negley Foxcroft. The waxed mustache danced furiously. "Why it's perfectly preposterous!"

Dave watched and listened with mixed emotions. Negley Foxcroft was acting as if in front of the TV cameras. His diction was good, his vocabulary impressive. But it had absolutely no effect on Mr. Codman, who was calmly chewing a blade of grass and occasionally pushing back his straw hat to scratch his bald head. If this keeps up, thought Dave, Negley

10

Foxcroft will get so mad he won't let me have the frame from his wrecked jalopy. And I'll have to buy one from some gyp of a junkman.

Dave was relieved to see the TV actor's performance fade from sheer lack of audience appreciation. Having failed to impress Mr. Codman, the actor asked if he could use the farmer's telephone to summon aid. Mr. Codman's answer to this was, "Why don't you broadcast a call for help over your TV station?" Whereupon the good farmer turned on his heel and departed with a squirt of saliva at a nearby rock.

That, thought Dave, will touch off another TV performance. Instead however, it turned Negley Foxcroft to Dave for help. Dave gladly supplied it, taking advantage of the favor to ask one in return—if he could unbolt the frame from the wreck before the junkman hauled it away.

"Why, of course, son," said Negley Foxcroft. "I'll even put that in writing." And having grandly performed an act of generosity before an appreciative audience of one, Negley Foxcroft regained his poise. As he once more twirled the waxed points of his mustache he announced that the youth of America was not yet lost.

His eloquence fell on deaf ears. Dave was interested only in the wreck's frame and the means of removing it. He would need help and he was sure it would not come from either Negley Foxcroft or Mr. Codman.

11

Chapter II

HELP came, in fact, from the Milltown Hot Rod Club, an organization Dave yearned to join. Dave belonged to no club, group, or gang, athletic or mechanical. At school he had tried out for the team in two sports, football and baseball. All in vain. In football he missed his blocks and tackles; in baseball he was poor at the plate and weak in the field. He just wasn't much of an athlete. Rejected, he drifted away from organized sports until his only contact with them was by radio and that only during the baseball season when the Yankees and Mickey Mantle were in a fight for the pennant.

So Dave had tried to join the Milltown Hot Rod Club. He had been impressed by its president, Max Werner, a good looking young man with a friendly grin and a hearty if slightly scoffing manner. "Well, so you want to join our club? That's fine, Dave, but where's your hot rod?"

He didn't have a hot rod, Dave was embarrassed to admit. But he had two friends in the club, Billy Forney and Ronnie Felton and they could testify that he, Dave Neil, was a good mechanic. "Swell," said president Max Werner. "The club welcomes members who are good mechanics but no exceptions can be made to the basic rule, Dave. Every candidate for membership must own a hot rod."

The candidate for membership must have looked dejected because Max Werner added, with a slap on the back, "If we can help in any way let us know. Once in a while we come across wrecks or jalopies that can be salvaged. Keep in touch with us, fella."

So Dave kept in touch. He helped Billy Forney with his pre-war Plymouth, he worked on Ronnie Felton's old Chevvie, and he admired Max Werner's Harley Davidson motorcycle much more than his hot rod, a V-8 shaped like a bathtub. In Dave's private opinion Max's hot rod was a "gook wagon" with all its shiny, superfluous equipment: searchlight, special horns, flashy fender flaps. But Dave had to admit that the V-8 had more pep than the other hot rods in the club. Just wait until I get mine, Dave thought, I'll show 'em.

It was a long wait but it was worth it. A Model A, free. And now a frame. Even president Max Werner

13

was impressed by Dave's good fortune. "I'll send someone over to help you, Dave," said Max over the phone and then added, "Maybe I'll even come myself."

And come himself he did, roaring down the road in his V-8, slamming on his brakes, skidding to a showy stop. Just as the president of a hot rod club should drive. Or should he? Dave wasn't sure. Anyway, here was Max swinging from behind the wheel of the V-8, swaggering over, nodding his peaked cap at the TV actor's wreck. "That the heap?"

"Yeah. Gee, it was swell of you to come."

Max grinned. "All in the day's work, Dave. Glad to help anyone interested in hot rods." Max hooked his thumbs in a wide belt studded with red and green reflectors. "You want to become a member of our club, Dave, and part of my job is to help candidates for membership, specially if they're good mechanics—and Bill Forney and Fonnie Felton say you're a darned good one, Dave."

"Gosh, that was nice of them," Dave mumbled. He could feel his face reddening.

"Sure," said Max. He smiled, slapped Dave on the back, "Well, let's get to work on that frame. Okay?"

"Yes," said Dave. He almost said, Yes sir.

They had tipped the wreck on its side and were unbolting the frame when Max suddenly said, "Watch it!"

A car was coming, a black sedan with a red light and a long aerial.

"It's the constable," said Max ominously.

"What constable?" asked Dave puzzled.

"The Branchville constable," said Max impatiently. "Didn't you realize you crossed the town line?"

"Oh," said Dave.

"He's a clown named Currie," added Max in a low voice. "And he hates hot rods. So watch what you say."

"Okay," said Dave still confused. But what difference did it make what he said? He wasn't doing anything wrong. Why was Max playing cops and robbers?

"Lookit the car he drives," Max was sneering. "A real Stupid Six. He couldn't catch a kid on a bike with that ash can. Lookit the whiskers he wears—just like Santa Claus. And believe me, Dave, he'd go faster with reindeer than he does with that Stupid Six."

Dave laughed a little. Pretty funny fellow, Max. And the constable did look a little like Santa Claus as he climbed out of the Stupid Six, revealing a sizable stomach exaggerated by a tight-fitting uniform.

" 'Lo, boys," he said, waddling across the road.

"Hi," said Max with a warning glance at Dave.

"Strippin' the wreck, ay?" asked the constable.

"Just taking the frame," said Dave quickly.

"Got permission?" said the constable, cocking his head to one side and tugging at his whiskers.

"Of course," said Max indignantly.

15

"Written or verbal?" said the constable tersely.

"I've got it in writing," said Dave, thankful for the TV actor's foresight.

Constable Currie carefully examined the crumpled paper Dave pulled out of his pocket. Apparently satisfied, the constable returned the document. "All right, boys, go ahead."

"Thanks, Officer," said Max sarcastically.

The constable ignored the sarcasm, tugged at his whiskers, nodded his constable's cap at the V-8, and said in a disapproving tone, "That's what you call a hot rod, ain't it?"

"It ain't a tricycle," said Max.

Dave gawked, half amused, half shocked at Max's flippancy.

"Humph," snorted Constable Currie, "Well, I'd say it was a sassy sort of car, jess like its owner."

Dave was surprised. The constable wasn't as dumb as Max had made him out to be. As for Max, he looked startled, indignant, but he said nothing; he let Constable Currie have the last word, "Hot rods are all right I guess, long's they obey the rules of the road. But if they come into my township speedin' and reckless drivin' I'll catch 'em and see that they git what they deserve."

"Not with that Stupid Six you won't," said Max Werner. But Dave noticed that Max made the remark only when the constable was well out of earshot. "He's got a nerve, that clown," Max went on, "always checkin' up on people. What's he think we are anyway, a couple of crooks?"

"Well, in a way you can't blame him," said Dave slowly. "It's his job, I guess, to check up on people."

"The law says you're innocent until you're proven guilty," declared Max. "That clown's got it twisted the wrong way. And that crack he made about me and my hot rod was uncalled for. Makes me sore. I've got a good mind to take a few extra parts off this wreck."

"Better get permission first," said Dave.

"Oh, I suppose so," said Max reluctantly. "Even if someone else swiped the parts Santa Claus would pin it on me."

"Could be," said Dave. He smiled, "Anyway I got a frame free."

"Yeah," said Max. "And it's a good thing you had written permission to take it else you'd be in jail."

"Maybe." Dave laughed at the absurdity of the thought and added jokingly, "But the hot rod club would bail me out, wouldn't it, Max?"

"If you were a member it would," said Max solemnly. "I go to bat for my boys and don't forget it." Then Max asked, "Listen, Dave, is that your bike leaning against that tree over there?"

"Yes," said Dave and again he felt ashamed for riding a bike and guilty for the shame. Was Max going to make some sarcastic crack about it?

17

Not at all. Max said, "Okay, Dave, get your bike, dump it in the back of my rod and I'll give yuh a ride home."

"Swell," said Dave. Max was really a nice guy. He tried a little too hard to be a bigshot, but that was more than balanced by his helpful, hearty manner. And could he drive his hot rod—wow! Listen to those tires scream in protest at that jack-rabbit start.

"Know what that's called, Dave?" Max had slowed down to explain his driving technique.

"What?" said Dave in an awed voice.

"That's what we call 'peeling rubber' at the hot rod club," said Max. He had shifted into first and, with his clutch in, was gunning the engine, *arroomm— arroomm.* "You jazz the accelerator like this, see? You rev it up real good. Now watch, I'm gonna snap out my clutch and tromp that gas pedal. Ready? Hold on!"

Wheeee. The rear tires wailed like banshees. The V-8 shot forward, rocked down the tar road. Dave sucked in his breath and held on. Max was some driver and this rod of his was pretty hot, no doubt about it. What's more, Max didn't seem to give a hoot about Constable Currie. The V-8 roared contemptuously past a stop sign at Chet Coley's filling station, skidded to the left, raced up the hill and rushed over the town line. Only then did Max ease up on the accelerator. As the car slowed down he spoke loudly, proudly, confidently,

18

"Pretty hot, ay Dave? Think I'll enter this rod in an out-of-state drag race. Hey! What the—"

Without warning the V-8's engine was missing. The hot rod that had roared so lustily was suddenly shivering and wheezing. And the cockiness drained out of Max Werner's face like rusty water out of an opened radiator.

In a desperate attempt to revive his favorite, Max tromped the accelerator. *Aroo-roof—woof.* The V-8 tried to growl powerfully and succeeded only in producing a pathetic bark. Scowling, red-faced, Max slowed down again. *Woof-ooff*—silence. A very loud silence. The gook wagon had collapsed.

Dave was embarrassed for Max. The president of the hot rod club seemed to sense the sympathy and brusquely rejected it; no one was going to feel sorry for Max Werner. Putting up a bold front, Max reached for a screw driver, swung out from behind the wheel as he muttered, "This'll just take a minute." Then he swaggered in search of the source of the trouble.

Dave followed discreetly. A big shot like Max wouldn't welcome interference, however helpful. So Dave kept quiet and watched. And saw an interesting performance.

"Ten to one it's the distributor," said Max. With a rough confident gesture he lifted the hood, leaned way in, snapped off the distributor's side caps, opened and closed the points. Then he straightened up and said,

19

"Humph, the distributor looks okay. I'll bet it's the carb." As confident as ever, he now attacked the carburetor with his screw driver.

Dave maintained his silence. It could be the carburetor. For that matter it could have been the distributor. On the other hand it might be something very simple like an empty gas tank. Gosh, that would be embarrassing to Max. It would really show him up as a dumbbell and Dave didn't want that to happen. For Max was a good guy even if he did try too hard to act like a big shot. And he was certainly a good enough mechanic to watch his gas gauge as well as his oil pressure. Still, simple things sometimes stopped engines—like a vacuum lock in the fuel line. The fuel line should certainly be inspected. Well, Max would probably think of it when he finished with the more complicated possibilities like the carburetor. He was doing a pretty thorough job on that carb, taking the spring off, the counterpin out.

Watching closely but quietly Dave was suddenly tempted to break his tactful silence. For Max was leaning over, puffing up his cheeks. And if he blew into that carb—

Whoosh. He did. And *Whoosh* the offended carburetor spat a faceful of gasoline at its tormentor.

Max staggered back, gasping, his hand to his face. He looked ridiculous but Dave saw nothing funny in the accident. He was thinking how stupid Max had been to blow in a carburetor. Apparently the president of the hot rod club didn't realize how temperamental engines could be.

Anyway, there he stood, wiping gasoline off his red face and sputtering like a wet spark plug. Realizing that he was staring at the victim and increasing his embarrassment, Dave stared instead at the engine. And picking up the thread of a former thought he examined the fuel line.

He found that the fuel line on the V-8 came out of the firewall from the gas tank as a steel tube, then changed to a flexible line of fabric and steel webbing. The flexible line, Dave knew, would have a rubber lining, not natural rubber which gas would rot, but synthetic stuff impervious to the chemical action of gasoline. These thoughts ran through Dave's head as his fingers lightly moved along this flexible line toward the firewall. When they came to the connection with the steel tube their pressure increased like a delicate machine that detects a flaw and signals its location. Sharp eyes responded to the signal; senses coordinated and flashed a message: loose fuel line connection.

Dave was pleased with his short successful search. But he concealed his elation from Max and said simply, "Looks like a loose connection on the fuel line. Got a couple of wrenches, Max?"

"Guess so," said Max unhappily.

"I think I'll need a nine-tenths and a one-half," said Dave quietly.

"Got some somewhere," mumbled Max, rummaging in the back of the bathtub. He finally brought forth a greasy, dilapidated wooden box with broken hinges.

A pretty sad-looking tool kit, Dave told himself, but it's none of my business. Maybe Max is one of those guys who is bored by the maintenance part of the hot rod game.

Dilapidated or not, the tool kit did have the size wrenches Dave needed to tighten the loose fuel line connection. It was an easy job for skillful fingers. And as Dave worked the wrenches, he thought how often the simple thing that caused the engine trouble was overlooked by ambitious hot rod owners who rushed to investigate the carburetor or the distributor, certain that their rods could not be immobilized by such obvious defects as empty gas tanks, unturned ignition switches, or loose fuel line connections.

"Want to try 'er now, Max?" Dave straightened up.

"Okay, Dave." Max had shaken off his embarrassment. He even managed a halfhearted grin, and a compliment given in a slightly scoffing tone. "Dave, the detective. Runs down any clue, however small. You'll get a promotion for this."

Dave chuckled as he carefully replaced the wrenches in the tool kit. "I don't care about the promotion. All I want is my own hot rod."

"And, by gosh, Dave, you're going to get it," said Max with a friendly slap on Dave's back. "Yes sir! And as soon as you do I'll be the first to welcome you into the Milltown Hot Rod Club."

"Thanks," said Dave, pleased at the turn events had taken. Max was not a brilliant mechanic but he was a friendly sort of fellow. Moreover he was the president of the hot rod club, the leader of the gang Dave yearned to join.

And talking of his hot rod club seemed to restore the damage done to Max's prestige by the contemptuous action of the carburetor. It was as if air were being pumped back into a tire that had been deflated. With each mention of the club, one of its members, or its activities, Max seemed to regain another pound of self-confidence. And he was soon back up at the high pressure which seemed normal to his personality.

This high pressure produced a plan which Max presented exuberantly—to drive his hot rod over the town line into Branchville and bait Constable Currie.

"Bait Constable Currie?" said Dave doubtfully.

"You bet!" cried Max. "Old Santa Claus thinks he's smart; he sets speed traps. Okay. I'll spring his traps, then outrace the constable to the town line."

"Gee," said Dave. Then he added, "Gosh, but Max, that's illegal."

"So what?" scoffed Max. "Think of the fun we'd get out of it."

23

"Hmm," said Dave. He didn't want to disagree openly with the president of a club he longed to join, but somehow baiting Constable Currie wasn't Dave's idea of fun.

"Pretty sharp scheme, isn't it?" cried Max, "'cause once you barrel across the town line on your road you can slam on your brakes and thumb your nose at the constable. His power of arrest ends right at the town line."

"Oh," said Dave and then forced a little enthusiasm. "Yes, it is a sharp scheme, Max."

"Sure it is," cried Max. "Hey, I've got an even better idea."

"What?" said Dave, and added to himself, a better idea? What made Max think that the first one was any good?

"I'll be the first to spring the speed traps," said Max boastfully, "because I'm the president of the club and I wouldn't ask any member to do anything I wouldn't do myself."

"Uh-huh," said Dave.

"But once I break the ice as leader," said Max, "then I can ask others to follow. Right?"

It was a rhetorical question. Without waiting for an answer Max babbled on, "So what I might do is to make this run an initiation stunt for new members. Wha' d'y' think of that, Dave?"

Dave didn't think much of it. But he didn't reveal

24

his true state of mind. What good would it do? Max was president of the club and obviously a president who was proud and jealous of his leadership. Dave was in no position to question it. He wasn't even a member of the club, because he didn't own a hot rod. That was his immediate objective, to put that Model A in running condition. That was why he had been so grateful for the free frame. It was a big step in the right direction. At least it seemed like a big step at the time.

Chapter III

Bᴜᴛ each step, Dave told himself that evening, was just a milestone along the road to an elusive destination. He felt like a traveler who has planned a trip which looks short on a road map but works out in actual daily mileage as an exacting and apparently endless journey. One milestone was the free frame, another was the new gas tank. The Model A's old gas tank was not only dilapidated—it was in the way. For by now Dave had streamlined his Model A, lowering the body, moving the firewall back and down, the radiator forward and down. The Model A was beginning to look like a real racing car but its gas tank stuck out like a sore thumb. For the gas tank of a Model A is near the dashboard and Dave's streamlining pushed the old tank into a position that would severely cramp the hot rod's driver.

Usually Dave avoided junkmen like the plague, picking up odd parts from friends, neighbors, or filling stations. But no one had the kind of gas tank he wanted. An automobile graveyard was indicated and the nearest was one run by an individual with the reassuring name of Honest Harold.

Honest Harold's automobile graveyard squatted beside a cement highway just one mile north of Milltown. Dave noticed the rotted wooden fence that had fallen down and was temporarily supported by a rope anchored to several wrecks. He stared suspiciously at Honest Harold's headquarters, a tar-papered shack protected by walls of assorted junk. It was ominously quiet in the graveyard. The only thing that moved was a blue wisp of smoke that curled up out of the shack's rusty chimney which Dave recognized as an old exhaust pipe. Suddenly a bell rang loudly. Shocked to a stop Dave realized that he had stepped on the kind of warning wire that filling stations use to signal the presence of customers.

A gravelly growl followed the bell's warning. "Wha' d'y' want?"

It was Honest Harold himself.

He was a mess, just like his junkyard. He was short, stout, and swarthy. A ragged beard grew in gray patches over his blotchy face. Small beady eyes peered craftily over two puffy pillows of blue-veined flesh. Two large discolored teeth clamped to a slimy dead cigar gave the fantastic impression that Honest Harold had been reincarnated as Bugs Bunny and, oblivious to his new personality, was gnawing on a stogie instead of a carrot.

When Dave found his tongue he said timidly, "I was looking for a gas tank."

"Garrumph." Honest Harold gave his version of a grunt. When that sound came forth Honest Harold seemed to change from hare to pig. A pig wallowing in his sty, thought Dave as he followed Honest Harold through a labyrinth of junk, over orange hills of rusting iron, black valleys of grease-soaked sand, entangling webs of rotting wire.

"Garrumph. Tank. Good condition." Honest Harold had miraculously detached a container from the clutter and was nudging it with a grease-stained shoe.

"How much?"

The two yellow tusks turned the slimy cigar. "Two bucks."

One for each tooth, thought Dave as Honest Harold added, "It would cost yuh five clams anywhere else, kid."

Two bucks, Dave thought. That's not too bad.

He bought it. It wasn't until he got it back to his barn that he discovered that the tank's gauge was missing and that its cap wouldn't stay on. And Honest Harold had said that it was in good condition. Honest

Harold—what a crook! Back that tank would go the next day.

But the next day it rained, hour after hour. Dave didn't move out of the barn except for meals and a few household chores. On the following day, however, he returned the tank to Honest Harold's junkyard. The warning bell rang and out of the shack, cigar, tusks, beady eyes, came the junkie. "Whatsa' matter?"

Dave gulped. "This tank's no good."

Honest Harold glared and growled. "Wha' d'y' mean it's no good?"

Bravely Dave told the junkie about the gauge and the cap, concluding, "I want my money back."

"Yuh want yuh money back?" Honest Harold's blotchy face turned purple, the yellow tusks bit savagely into the cigar. "You crazy, kid? You outta yuh mind? Deals are final after twenty-four hours. You shoulda' brought it back yesterday. Today is too late."

"But it was raining yesterday," Dave protested and as soon as he said it realized it sounded ridiculous.

"Rainin'!" Honest Harold's tusks almost dropped their cigar. "Whatsa matter, afraid to getcha feet wet?" the junkie snorted. "Jiesel-diesel! What gives wit da younger generation dese days? No guts—no guts at all."

"I want my money back," Dave persisted.

"Yuh needle's stuck, sonny." The cigar cocked belligerently. "Yuh playin' da same old tune. I told yuh, deals are final after twenty-four hours."

29

"You did not!" cried Dave half angry, half afraid, his face white, his fists clenched. It was on the tip of his tongue to say, I'm going to call the cops. But the Milltown police, Dave knew, were sworn enemies of the Milltown Hot Rod Club. So Dave quickly changed his rescuer from policeman to lawyer. "Listen, if you don't give me my money back I'll sue you."

Heen-nyaaa.

Had a billy goat blaated, a horse whinnied? No. Honest Harold had laughed, the strangest, eeriest laugh Dave had ever heard.

"Listen kid," the cigar wobbled, the beady eyes glittered, "take my advice. Never sue nobody. All yuh do is give yuh money to lawyers."

"Yeah?" said Dave doubtfully. "Well just the same . . ."

"Listen sonny." Honest Harold's gravelly growl suddenly purred. "You t'ink I'd gyp yuh? I wouldn't do dat. Listen, we'll work out some kinda deal." The cigar wobbled in a friendly way.

"Now I'll tell yuh what I'll do for yuh, kid." Honest Harold once more led the way, burrowed into a pile, uncovered a gas tank. "Now here's a real wonderful buy. This here tank is in perfect condish. Got a good gauge, good top; it's in A-1 shape inside and out. Tell yuh what I'll do, kid. You turn in your tank, gimme three more clams and this beauty is yours."

30

Dave squatted, examined the tank, tested its cap. No doubt about it, this definitely was a better tank. Dave straightened up. "What kind of a tank is this?" he asked.

Honest Harold chewed his cigar. "It's a Chevvy tank but it come off a Model A—yuh know how mixed up these jalopies get with kids like you workin' on 'em."

"Hmm," said Dave, "what happened to the Model A?"

Heen—nyaaa. Honest Harold laughed, the fiendish cackle of a vulture who thrives on fatalities. "Slight accident. Dumb driver. Tried to chop down a tree."

Jeepers, said Dave to himself, that sounds like the same car I got the frame from. Gosh, now I have to pay five bucks for the gas tank. What a gyp. He sighed. But at least the frame was free.

Honest Harold's laugh turned into a growl. "I lost dough on da deal, kid. I paid fifteen bucks for the wreck, plus labor, towin', breakin' it up and so forth. And the crook who sold it to me—know what he does —he let some kids steal the frame! How about dat?" Honest Harold's tusks released the cigar and guided a stream of brown saliva at a broken headlight. "I tell yuh sonny, yuh gotta watch yuh step dese days. Everybody's out t' gyp yuh."

"You can say that again," said Dave. And to himself he added, I'm getting out of here before I lose my shirt.

As Dave continued his work on the Model A each obstacle met and overcome produced a fine feeling of satisfaction. Summer's heat cooled under autumn's frosts and many of Dave's classmates played football for Milltown High. Dave remembered how envious he had once been of classmates who could get off a long punt, throw a slick pass, or run elusively with the ball. It had all been beyond Dave and he had suffered for his want of athletic ability. No longer. He had his Model A; his hot rod was on its way; he would show his skill in another field.

Hardened by the experience painfully acquired at Honest Harold's, Dave found a second auto graveyard and, after haggling, bargaining, testing, picked up an amazing variety of useful equipment. In this second junkyard Dave bought a water pump and generator from a '36 Hudson, a cowl from an old Ford roadster, and the cheapest piece of equipment of all, a wind screen, a flimsy but serviceable pane detached from a broken-down motorcycle—cost, fifty cents.

Dave carefully kept track of each purchase, a description of the item, and its price. He was pleased to see that his bank account, strengthened by the summer job in the filling station, could stand the drain. Only one thing really worried him—tires. The original Model A had two nineteen-inch tires with hopelessly cracked sidewalls and bare spots showing on surfaces long worn smooth. Dave decided to buy sixteen-inch wheels and tires with broader surface for better traction. Not new tires but sturdy retreads. That would be the biggest expense of the project and Dave postponed it till spring—no use putting tires on the Model A while it stood immobile in the barn.

The only thing moving in the barn that winter was Dave; he had to move to keep warm. There was no danger of the Model A's radiator freezing and cracking for there was no water in it, but Dave's fingers almost froze and cracked. And when a wrench slipped and freezing fingers banged against cold steel, the pain was excruciating. Dave's nose always seemed to be running in an irritating, tickling way and the toes of his feet ached, grew numb, and then burned as they came back to life. But he kept on working. There were a few bitterly cold days when he had to suspend operations but there was never much more than a moment when he considered abandoning the project. The Model A, its growth and development into a hot rod, had become the very reasons for Dave's existence, the greatest goal to which he had ever aspired.

Chapter IV

THE goal was reached. Early in the spring Dave road tested the Model A. He did it all by himself because he wasn't sure what kind of a performance the model was going to give, and if it were a poor one he preferred it to be private. But it wasn't a poor performance. Dave was delighted with the way the Model A ran. And his first impulse was to race down to the hot rod club which had just reopened and proudly blurt out the wonderful news to Max Werner, Ronnie Felton, Billy Forney.

But on second thought Dave decided on a more subtle presentation of the news. It would be more effective, he decided, to drop in at the club as if nothing had happened, wait for the right moment,

then make the announcement. It should be a sensational surprise because Dave had kept his Model A
under wraps. And the Milltown winter had pulled
another blanket of privacy over the progress of the
project. Winter in Milltown sharply curtailed the activities of the hot rod club. In the first place the
shack that served as club headquarters had no heat,
which chilled the theoretical side of the club. And in
the second place the roads around Milltown in winter
were often snowy or icy, which was discouraging to
the practical side of the club, even to drivers as in-
trepid as Max Werner.

There was one more reason why Dave wanted to
spring a surprise on the hot rod club, and the reason
was the club's leader. Since Max had helped free the
frame from the car wrecked on Mr. Codman's elm,
Dave had changed his opinion of the president of the
hot rod club. At first Dave had been an admirer of Max
Werner; Dave had even imitated Max's manner of
dress, the peaked cap with the shiny visor worn at a
jaunty angle, the tight blue jeans, the leather jacket.
Dave couldn't afford to buy the wide, garish, reflector-
studded "kidney belt" which Max wore so proudly, but
Dave had succeeded in growing long fuzzy sideburns
in front of his ears. He had been deeply impressed by
Max Werner—at first. But when Max blew into his
V-8's carburetor with explosive results, some of Dave's
awe had ebbed; mechanically Max wasn't very bright.

And Dave had discovered, as the hot rod season drew to a close, that he was deficient in other respects.

It happened on an unusually warm Saturday night in the late fall. In the afternoon Milltown High had won the last football game of the season. That night the victorious team was feted at a dance in the school's gym. The hot rodders, led by Max Werner, attended the game but shunned the victory dance. "We'll put on our own kind of celebration!" Max Werner cried; and, peeling rubber, he had started a wild and woolly game called Follow the Leader. The rules of this game were simple. Max led, the others followed and anyone who dropped out was scornfully called "chicken."

Dave rode as a passenger in Billy Forney's pre-war Plymouth. Dave was excited; Billy Forney was carried away completely. Hands high on the wheel, shoulders hunched over it Billy talked without turning his head, "Lookit that guy drive! Ain't he somepin, Dave?"

Max had just skidded around a corner and sailed through a stop sign.

"Yeah," Dave agreed, "Max is quite a driver." But gosh, suppose another car had been tearing down that highway when the hot rod club, led by Max Werner, roared through the stop sign?

Dave kept the question to himself. He knew it would be futile to ask it of Billy Forney. Billy had left this world to enter another one of sensational, intoxicating excitement. "Yuh gotta hand it t' Max," Billy raved.

"Once he gets behind the wheel of that V-8 he's in a class by himself."

Dave held on and said nothing. Max was certainly a sensational driver but his was the kind of driving that could be hard on a car. He ground his gears too often and he must have already worn half the tread off his rear tires. Nevertheless he was clearly the leader and faithfully followed by boys like Billy Forney. What was Billy saying now over the sound of the Plymouth's engine?

"—Max always drives better after he has a few beers." Billy's voice was hoarse with awe and admiration.

A few beers? That was really stupid, Dave thought. Reckless driving was bad enough but drunken driving was—

"Lookit that guy wind it out!" Billy was beginning to sound hysterical.

They were roaring along the straight stretch of a moonlit back road. It was a hard dirt road with an uneven surface, a series of ridges that reminded Dave of a flat stretch of sand that has been rippled by waves. Taken at slow speed this rippled road bumped a car along like a trotting horse jouncing its rider. At high speed the bumping disappeared as it does when a slow trot turns into a smooth gallop. But the risk of skidding increased with reduced traction as the rear tires spun from one ripple to the next. It was a little like driving on ice. Dave could feel the slipperiness beneath him. And it was an uneasy feeling. Billy Forney, Dave thought, was foolish to play follow the leader on this kind of road. It was too slippery even here on this straight stretch, and as Dave remembered the road there were two curves coming up, the second sharper than the first.

"Wow! Listen to that, Dave!"

There was a piercing scream of protest from the tires of the V-8 as Max careened around a corner. Suddenly the V-8 was skidding on two wheels. Would it turn over? Dave held his breath. He relaxed as the V-8 righted itself, straightened out, then shot ahead with a belligerent roar from its twin tail pipes.

"Whewww!" Billy Forney let out a long loud sigh of awe, fright, and relief.

Dave spoke over a pounding heart. "Max was lucky. If he takes the next curve that fast he'll be in real trouble."

"Gee," was all Billy Forney could say. Sobered by Max's skid Billy eased up on the throttle and carefully negotiated the corner Max had taken so recklessly. But then he tromped the gas pedal again because the other hot rods were catching up and he was in danger of being passed on the short straight stretch that led to the second, sharper corner.

Billy wasn't passed however, so he and Dave had a clear unobstructed view of the way Max Werner and his V-8 took the second corner. And the picture would live forever in their memories.

For Max went into the most sensational skid they had ever seen. With a wild wail from its tires, like a blast from bagpipes, the V-8 skidded around until it faced its astonished audience. Then with the arrogance of its owner, it seemed to thumb its nose at the two shocked faces staring through the windshield of the Plymouth before shooting over the shoulder of the road, miraculously missing two trees, then bouncing, banging and crunching to a stop on an unploughed field.

"Holy jumpin' catfish!" Billy Forney released the expression in a hoarse whisper. And as he guided the Plymouth to a stop he added "Boy! What driving! D'y' ever see anything like it? Gee, the way Max squeezed his hot rod between those two trees—wow!"

"Yeah," said Dave. But was it skill or just dumb luck? Never mind. The important thing was to see if Max had survived, thought Dave, jumping out of the Plymouth and running toward the V-8.

Max had survived. He was even able to grin feebly and say in a shaky voice, "Some stunt, ay Dave?"

"You okay, Max?"

"Sure. Not a scratch."

The others came running up and Dave noticed that with his awed gang around him Max quickly regained his self-confidence; the feeble grin grew strong, the voice firm. "Okay, fellas, let's put the show back on the road."

Back on the road? Dave repeated the question to himself. Well, the star of the show was off the road all right. That was certain. But wouldn't it be a good idea to close the show before somebody got hurt?

Obviously Max didn't think so. He was swaggering around the V-8 inspecting it for damage, a very superficial inspection, Dave thought, concerned mostly with the condition of the hot rod's tires. If I were Max, thought Dave, I'd crawl under that heap with a flashlight and check it from one axle to the other.

Max had no such earthy intentions. He was anxious, as he said, to put the show back on the road. And as soon as he had checked the tires and found no flats he swung back behind the wheel of the V-8, stabbed at the starter, jazzed the accelerator—*arroom arroom.* The faithful V-8 responded with a roar of its engine and Max shouted, "Okay, fellas, stand back! I'm gonna peel rubber!"

Peel rubber here? thought Dave doubtfully.

Arroom. The V-8's engine roared. *Whaaannngg.* The rear tires dug into the field. *Whoosh-whup.* The tires slowed, stopped; the hot rod was stuck in the mud.

But nobody mocked Max. And he was surprisingly good-natured as he once more summoned his followers to his side and said, "Gimme a push, will you, fellas? Guess I'll have to back out of this bog."

Arroom arrooom. Max jazzed the accelerator, rocked the V-8 in the rut and then with the help of strenuous pushing from the front hurtled the hot rod back onto the road.

"Thanks a lot, fellas. And now—follow me!" With a roar from the twin pipes and a scream from the rear tires Max peeled rubber and rocketed down the road.

"Come on, Dave!" Billy Forney was running toward the Plymouth. Dave followed in time to hear Billy say, "Gee, that guy Max Werner sure has guts. If I had skidded off the road like that I would've been so scared I would've walked home. How about you, Dave?"

Dave smiled, "Well, at least I would have driven home slowly."

"Sure," said Billy, shifting gears. "I would've walked, you would've crawled. And that's why neither one of us'll ever be president of the Milltown Hot Rod Club."

"I suppose so," said Dave. And what did it matter anyway? Max was the guy who wanted to be the big shot. And he sure had a big-shot personality, hail-fellow-well-met, reckless, courageous. And although he was too reckless and his courage was a little on the show-off side, nevertheless the members of the—

"Gol blast that Felton character!" Billy Forney was shouting about Ronnie Felton, who had suddenly roared by, then cutting in sharply, forced Billy to ease up on the accelerator to avoid locking fenders with the Chevvy.

"That's a heck of a way t' drive," Billy complained.

Dave agreed. In fact, many of the ways the hot rods had been driven on this exciting night had seemed like wrong ways to him. But if you played "follow the leader" you had to do what the leader did. And if the leader were a guy like Max Werner, you ignored stop signs and drove too fast on skiddy roads.

A loud noise shattered Dave's stream of thought, a rapid-fire noise like that made by a kid running a stick along a picket fence—bang-bang-bang-bang-bang.

"Jumpin' Judas!" cried Billy Forney. "Ronnie Felton's thrown a rod."

Dave disagreed. Listening closely he said, "That racket isn't coming from Ronnie's car—it's the V-8 up ahead; Max has burned out a bearing."

"How d'you know?" said Bill sharply.

"Because that's the noise that burned out bearings make," said Dave. He was speaking quietly, calmly, like a doctor sure of his diagnosis. And he added, "I'll bet he knocked a hole in his oil pan."

"Knocked a hole in his oil pan?" said Billy excitedly.

"When he skidded off the road into that field," said Dave calmly, "he probably hit a big rock. That would do it, too. Max was going pretty fast when he ploughed into that field."

"Yeah," said Billy, impressed by Dave's analysis. "Gee whiz," Billy shook his head and then said, "Listen, Dave, the noise is slowin' up. Guess he's stopping."

"He'd better," said Dave dryly.

"Holy crow," said Billy hoarsely. He slowed down. "You mean he lost all his oil?"

"Probably," said Dave in a matter-of-fact tone. "And that would do plenty of damage."

"Sure," said Billy, and added quickly, "like what?"

"Burn out the bearings," said Dave, "making that noise we heard. It might also score the crankshaft, score the cylinder walls, and burn out the rings."

"Jumpin' Judas," said Billy, "think of the repair job."

"I wouldn't want to," said Dave. "It'll mean regrinding the crankshaft, reboring the cylinder walls, replacing the rings."

"Gee," said Billy wagging his head. "Max sure has his work cut out for him."

"He sure has," said Dave, recalling the clumsy way Max had attacked something as simple as a loose fuel line connection. But then there was always the possibility that Max could talk a good mechanic into helping him with the job because Max could, when he felt like it, act in an ingratiating way. It was all part of his personality—the personality of a politician, Dave decided.

Billy Forney broke in on Dave's thought. They had

pulled up behind the V-8 and in their headlights could see Max talking things over with Ronnie Felton. "Max doesn't seem downhearted," said Billy, "he's taking it in his stride." Billy switched off his ignition and Dave could hear Max talking loudly, "It happens to the best of us; just one of the breaks of the game. If you take chances like I do, Ronnie, you have to accept the good with the bad."

"That's right, Max," Ronnie Felton was saying as Billy Forney hurried up in time to nod in agreement. Dave just listened and heard Max say, "I'm not gonna let a little thing like this cramp my style. While my rod is in the repair shop I'm gonna lead you guys on my motorcycle."

"Attaway Max," said Ronnie Felton.

"We'll follow," said Billy Forney.

Dave said nothing. For all he cared Max could lead the club on a velocipede. Dave was interested in automobile engines, not club politics. He was bothered by the way Max mishandled his hot rod, ignored the oil gauge on his dashboard, neglected to get out and get under. But that, Dave figured, was Max's funeral.

Dave wanted only to belong to the club. And mechanic or not, Max was still president.

Chapter V

SEVERAL months later Max Werner was still the president of the hot rod club. And his V-8 was still being repaired—it would be ready to run any day now, Max had said for the last thirty days. Meanwhile the president of the hot rod club retained his position by performing daring feats on his motorcycle, and describing them graphically at hot rod meetings.

At first Dave had listened to these tales with grudging admiration. But at the meeting in mid-March, he listened uneasily, aware that he was tiring of Max Werner's boastful stories.

Max was in fine fettle at this meeting. It was midnight, but the subject of his speech still held his audience spellbound. For Max was describing how he had made a fool out of Constable Currie in enemy territory, over the town line in Branchville.

"Santa Claus set a speed trap for me," said Max scornfully.

Billy Forney laughed out loud. "Santa Claus," he echoed, "that's good."

Apparently the other members of the hot rod club agreed. They laughed, snickered, smiled. Only Dave failed to react favorably or flatteringly.

"So Santa Claus springs this speed trap and starts after me," Max continued. "Boy, was he in for a surprise!" Max snorted derisively, picked up a can of beer, expertly punched two holes in it, tipped his head back, drank.

The club members listened and watched in an atmosphere heavy with awe and adulation. But Dave's attitude placed him outside of this atmosphere. And the heavier the awe and adulation the less impressed Dave became. It was silly of Billy Forney and Ronnie Felton to stand there goggle-eyed at Max Werner's recital. How much more interesting it would be to have a discussion on an improved engine, the Model A for example.

He had put the finishing touches to it that very day in the barn behind the cottage where he lived with his mother. His final touch had been to remove the fan, which added a little more horsepower to the engine. The results had delighted him. The Model A now had more power and did not overheat in spite of the absence of the fan. It was ready. For what? A road race against Max Werner's V-8? No. The V-8 was still out of action. Well, then, how about a race against Ronnie Felton's streamlined Chevvy or Billy Forney's pre-war Plymouth? No. The competition was not hot enough because neither Ronnie nor Billy knew enough about engines.

Dave hesitated. He had meant to keep his Model A secret, save its exciting power for something really important like an out-of-state drag race. But Max Werner's boastful arrogance flushed the Model A out from cover. Before Dave could stop himself he had blurted out the news he meant to keep concealed, "I'll bet my Model A could—." Could what? Alarmed at the implications of that question Dave choked off the challenge, thinking, Gosh, I'm talking just like Max Werner. And besides I want to keep my hot rod under wraps.

But it was too late; the secret was out. Dave was like the timid novice who makes an injudicious jump at the end of a diving board and is horrified to find himself springing into space. Annoyed at being interrupted, Max seized upon Dave's half-hearted, half-finished remark, "You can do *what* with your Model A, Dave?"

"Oh nothin'," Dave mumbled.

"Humph." Max was scornful. "That's what I

thought." Max swirled his can of beer, tipped his head back, drank.

Billy Forney spoke up, "Gee, Dave, have you really got your Model A running?"

Dave nodded, feeling that a gesture would be safer than words with Max waiting to pounce.

But he pounced anyway. Max slapped Dave on the back and grinned, but his words were not congenial, "You're sure it's a hot rod, Dave, and not just a candidate for the soap box derby?"

Dave saw red. "Listen!" he blurted out. "My hot rod runs, Max—that's a lot more than yours does."

Max Werner reacted instantly, irritably. "All right, wise guy, if your heap is so hot, run it over the town line into Branchville and outrace Constable Currie."

Dave was staggered. He stalled for time, pointing at himself and saying in a shocked voice, "Who—me?"

"Yes—you." Max pointed another finger at Dave's cringing chest.

Dave tried to rally his retreating thoughts. "But why should I be the sucker?"

Max smiled sardonically. "You mean the chicken."

Dave reddened, "I'm not chicken and you know it."

Max continued to smile. "O.K. Then why are you balking?"

"Because you said all I had to do to join the club was to get a hot rod—and I got it." Dave looked at Billy Forney and Ronnie Felton, imploring support. But they were listening to Max Werner who was now talking in his confident president-of-the-club tone, "Oh, but that was the old rule, Dave. Now all new members have to undergo an initiation stunt." Max smiled unctuously. "I told you this was going to happen months ago, Dave. Matter of fact, you were the first person I talked to about it—remember?"

Dave stalled again. "Initiation stunt?" he said in a faint voice.

"Sure," said Max confidently. "Every club has initiation stunts these days." Max grinned. "You join a fishing club, you catch a fish; join a shooting club, you shoot a duck or somepin'. Well, this is a hot rod club so new members got to show what they can do with their hot rods. And a swell way to show what they can do is by outracin' that clown of a constable in Branchville, springin' his speed traps. Fair enough, fellas?" Max suddenly rasped at his followers. And, as usual, they nodded or murmured in agreement.

"And don't forget," Max added in a softer tone, "that I was the first to outrace that clown of a constable. I'll never ask any of you to do anything I wouldn't do myself. And so I hereby now propose—" Max turned pompous—"that this initiation stunt become an official rule right here and now, and I want one of you to make a resolution to that effect."

Dave hardly heard the resolution proposed by Ronnie Felton, seconded by Billy Forney, that all new members must undergo the initiation suggested by the president. For Dave knew now that the die was cast. An illegal escapade had become an official initiation rite and Dave had to go through with it or be disgraced in the eyes of all.

Max knew this, the club members knew it. Dave was on the spot, the center of a highly critical circle. And, though Max smiled, his voice was a taunt as he said, "O.K. Dave, this puts it squarely up to you and your rattletrap."

Rattletrap! That marvelous, wonderful Model A on which he had put so many weeks, months of nail-breaking, back-spraining, savings-draining work. Gosh, when you worked on a car like that, you started with affection and ended with love. Dave loved that Model A and no one was going to call it a rattletrap and get away with it—not even Max Werner.

His moist fists clenched, Dave swept the group with a challenging glare. "Come on," he cried, "I'll show you what a real hot rod can do!"

They were delighted to follow, jeering and laughing as they trooped noisily out of the club to start up their motorcycles and jalopies with loud raucous bursts from the exhausts and the usual complaints from disturbed neighbors. An old man in an undershirt appeared at a second-story window and shouted, "Get those ash cans out of here!"

"Okay, gramps, we're goin'," yelled Max Werner,

and loud laughs from the members of the group
mingled with the racket from exhausts. Then Max
Werner twisted the hand throttle on his Harley-Davidson and with a contemptuous roar led the little caval-
cade through the darkened streets of Milltown, past
the general store and wire factory and on up the hill
to the cottage where Dave lived with his mother.

For a moment Dave was worried about his mother.
If she were at home there might be embarrassing
questions about where he was going and why. Dave's
mother didn't like Max Werner and his influence on
Dave and had said as much. So Dave feared a scene.
But his mother had gone to the movies with the Millers,
said a note in the front door. That settled that. Relieved, Dave led the way behind the cottage to the
barn where the Model A waited. His hands trembled
with excitement as he unsprung the padlock on the
old wooden door, rolled it back on its squeaking
trolley, switched on a pale yellow cobwebbed light.
Then he stepped up to a long, low, canvas-covered
object and, like a sculptor unveiling his masterpiece,
pulled off the canvas and anxiously awaited the reaction of the audience.

It was favorable, very favorable. The members of
the hot rod club who had pressed noisily and derisively
at Dave's back, stared in awed silence at the car he
had created. It was impressive. It looked like a racing
car. It wasn't a gook wagon like Max Werner's crippled

V-8. Nor did it have stock car lines like Ronnie Felton's Chevvy or Billy Forney's Plymouth. It was more than a hot rod—it was a racing car. It was low, stripped, and streamlined. It was impressive and the members of the hot rod club obviously thought so; Dave could tell by the things they said and the way they looked.

All, of course, except Max Werner. He hooked both thumbs in his elegant, reflector-studded kidney belt, cocked his peaked cap to one side, and said, "Well, it ain't bad lookin', Dave, but"—he smiled sardonically—"will it run?"

"Wha' d' y' mean will it run?" Dave was indignant. "'Course it'll run." He grabbed his driving goggles from a nail on the wall and hurriedly swung his body behind the steering wheel, so hurriedly that he painfully banged his knee against the steering shaft. He also dislodged the front seat which consisted of a battered cushion borrowed from a porch chair and placed flatly on the Model A's floorboards.

"Careful, Dave," jibed Max, "it might bite."

Nobody laughed, Dave noted gratefully. He switched on the ignition and pushed in the clutch pedal so that the battery would have no extra work to turn the transmission. Then with jaws set, heart thumping, he pressed the starter button. It should start—it must start!

Arrurruh—rurruh—rurruh went the starter. And suddenly, wonderfully, it caught, sparked, exploded;

the inimitable throaty roar of a Model A burst upon Dave's delighted ears; the eager power of the engine he had assembled throbbed through the accelerator.

As he shifted into first, Dave cast a proud glance over the group that had followed him so skeptically and derisively into his crude workshop. The derision and skepticism had given way to interest, then admiration. The appearance of the Model A, the loud confident sound of its engine had changed Dave's status from just another follower in the hot rod club to a real member.

Chapter VI

DAVE would never forget that ride through the warm spring night, the feel of the car he had built, the sound of its engine and, above all, the fact that for the first time he was the center of attention. He, Dave Neil, was going to race his hot rod against a constable's car; and the risk and excitement made Dave's hands sweat on the steering wheel as he double-clutched and shifted into second for the steep hill that led to route 53. On route 53 lay the town line and beyond it the realm of Constable Currie.

It was not a very clear night. There was a moon but it appeared only fleetingly through murky, ragged clouds. Dave was glad that the generator from the '36 Hudson kept the battery's juice flowing strongly into new headlight bulbs. With a glance in his rear vision mirror he compared the strong white glow of his headlights with the feeble flickering from the hot rods that followed. They weren't real hot rods—they were jalopies; they just weren't in the same class with this Model A.

Dave watched his headlights probe around a curve and pick up the glass reflectors set in a post-and-cable fence. Sweeping on, the headlights caught the gleaming eyes of a cat cowering beside the road. Beyond the cat was the luminous paint of the highway sign that marked the intersection with route 53. And the marking on the sign said in big broad letters "STOP."

Automatically Dave put his foot on the brake. And then he remembered the kind of procession he was leading. What would the hot rodders, particularly Max Werner, think if he, Dave Neil, obeyed that stop sign? Did it matter? No. Well, yes, on initiation night it mattered. So Dave took his foot off the brake and putting it back on the accelerator swung out onto route 53 with a spurt that made his tires sob. Behind him horns honked approvingly at his defiance of the law.

The Model A was now on a well-paved two-lane highway and Dave asked his car for speed. It responded with a roar, raucous, confident. It was more than just a noise, it was a paean played on twin exhaust pipes, the sweetest song Dave had ever heard, doubly sweet because his mechanical mind knew that the two exhausts added power to the engine by cutting down back pressure.

So Dave sat proudly behind the wheel enjoying all the wonderful sensations of fast driving in an open car. The night air slipped over the cowl, brushed softly over his goggles, rushed excitingly past his ears. It was wonderful and the realization that he had put this hot rod together, part by part, added immeasurably to the thrill of the ride.

Suddenly the sharp staccato noise of a motorcycle engine blatted discordant notes into the sweet symphony played by the Model A. Dave jerked his head to the left. A cop? No. Max Werner on his Harley-Davidson. Dave experienced a feeling of relief that changed immediately into one of displeasure. For Max was yelling at Dave to slow down, that they were almost at the boundary that separated Branchville from Milltown.

Dave's hands had dried on the wheel as he drove along route 53. Now they began to sweat again. The time had come for him to make good on his boast— that he could spring Constable Currie's speed trap with the Model A. For just a few yards ahead on the right side of the road there stood, like a silent sentinel, the sign in luminous paint. And this time Dave read all of it: "BRANCHVILLE. Incorporated 1825. TOWN LINE."

Tonight that sign had a significant meaning. And as Dave read it in the glare of his headlights he felt a strange clash of feelings. He didn't want to break the law and show up Constable Currie. He really wanted to show up Max Werner; the leader of a hot rod club had no business boasting about feats performed on a motorcycle. But was this the right way to do it? Dave didn't have time to answer the question for he was immediately asked one by an arrogant voice.

"Got a cut-out on this rod?" Max Werner had parked his motorcycle and swaggered back to the waiting Model A. With his goggles pushed back up on his forehead and his gauntlets coming off slowly Max looked like a motorcycle cop about to make an arrest. As he watched this figure approach, Dave realized that there was some real fear in his attitude toward Max. Dave didn't like that fear to be there and he had a sudden strong desire to stamp it out. The thought occurred to him that a triumph in the coming contest with Constable Currie might be a good way to get rid of that fear.

But all Dave said over the engine's idle, was, "Sure, I've got a cut-out. Want to hear it?"

"Not now," said Max, "but I've got a plan for it."

Dave frowned. Max always had a plan. That was one of the reasons he was the leader of the hot rodders. Unfortunately many of his plans involved misdemeanors and the hot rodders had earned a reputation as the terrors of the local highways. But Dave had to admit that Max had been clever about his law breaking; most of the flagrant violations took place in the township of Branchville at the expense of Constable Currie.

"Santa Claus'll be lyin' in wait for you," Max was saying as he leaned patronizingly on Dave's Model A, "so you can take your heap and—"

"Heap." Dave bridled at the word. In his opinion "heap" should be used only in speaking of inferior hot rods—there was nothing inferior about the Model A. Nor was there anything inferior about Max Werner's plan, Dave reluctantly admitted, as he listened.

There would be a trial run. "Just like a regular road race," Max said. Dave would cross the town line, go down the short steep hill, open his cut-out, and roar past Chet Coley's filling station. Constable Currie would in all probability be sitting in the station chewing the fat with Chet Coley and drinking birch beer, a drink which Max pronounced with rich scorn. Constable Currie would bang down the bottle and cry, "Them durned hot rodders are at it again!"

Max laughed and Dave found himself smiling. Caught up in the conspiracy he even boasted a little, "By the time Santa Claus gets to his wagon I should be halfway to the town hall."

"Sure," Max agreed. "And Santa Claus'll be waitin'

for you when you come back. That's where the road race'll come in."

"Where d'y' think he'll be waitin', Max?" Dave's question was husky with nervous excitement.

"I've got it all figured out," said Max pompously. "But wait a second. Here comes the gang. I want to line 'em up and brief 'em."

A noise like a barnyard being raided by a fox heralded the arrival of the rest of the Milltown hot rodders. Dave listened disdainfully to the discordant sounds of the engines. What a bunch of jalopies; not a real hot rod among 'em.

Max had swaggered to the middle of the road, the glass studs on his kidney belt reflecting the glare of the oncoming headlights. Imperiously he stopped the cars, directed them to parking places. Then the plan was unfolded to all.

Max on his motorcycle was going to act as a scout. He would reconnoiter, spot the location of Constable Currie's speed trap, which would probably be at either of two intersections on route 53—Irv Lockwood's farmhouse, screened by tall evergreens, or Hurlbutt's cider mill. Using dirt road short cuts, Max would relay his information to Dave by signaling with his headlight from a point of vantage on the long steep S-turn hill, Dead Man's Hill, which led down to the stone bridge and the center of Branchville. If Max's headlight gave one long flash Constable Currie's speed trap would be set at the cider mill, the intersection nearer the top of Dead Man's Hill. If it blinked twice the Constable would be hiding behind the screen of evergreens at the Lockwood farmhouse. Knowing the exact location of the speed trap would give Dave a definite advantage as he prepared for the contest with the constable.

As the group listened to the plan unfold there were murmurs of admiration, nods of approval. Max was a planner all right; no wonder he was the leader.

These thoughts allowed Dave to accept without protest or criticism Max's plan for the escapade. Besides it was a good plan—it had everything worked out nicely, the roaring ride past the filling station that would provoke the constable, the signaling that would pinpoint the location of the speed trap.

"And from there on, Dave, it's up to you." Max's hand was on Dave's shoulder, Max's tone was patronizing; his whole attitude suggested that the scheme was perfect and that only some shocking blunder on Dave's part would spoil the master plan.

Dave adjusted his goggles, switched on the ignition. He was about to press the starter button when Max said in a low confidential tone, "Listen, Dave, I've had a lot more experience than you with stunts like these. If I was you I'd play it this way. Roll up to that speed trap fast, see, but with the clutch in so your engine'll be quiet. Then throw the cut-out switch and shift into

60

second. Then rev 'er up and really wind it out. Now of course you might not wanna—"

Barrumph. Dave had pressed the starter button and, like a network radio engineer cutting off a local station, stopped Max's flow of condescending conversation. "Rev 'er up—wind it out." Not the phrases but the way Max used them irked Dave—the knowing chatter without the real mechanical knowledge—that was Max all over.

Scowling, Dave shifted into first and wound up the engine, right foot jazzing the accelerator, left foot pressing the clutch to the floor. Suddenly he peeled rubber. As he snapped out his clutch the revved up engine turned the rear tires so fast that they spun without gripping. And while they spun they screamed in protest. As they took hold they hurled the Model A forward in a sensational start that brought admiring shouts from the Milltown hot rodders and completely silenced their leader.

A few yards down the road Dave took his foot off the gas, shifted into second, and gallantly waved good-by. He knew why he could be so casual; he was behind the wheel of his Model A and his car gave him an intoxicating feeling of power. This feeling obscured his conscience, which had been trying to register a protest against this illegal initiation stunt.

Dave's conscience could not prevail against the intoxicating feeling of power that thrived on speed and sound: the brash roar of the Model A, the rush of cool night air, the high-pitched hum of racing tires, and now another exciting sound as Dave guided the Model A down the short steep hill toward Chet Coley's filling station—the loud confident coughing of the Model A as it backed off its pipes.

Dave was very proud of those twin tail pipes. They were not superfluous decorations like the flashy fender flaps on Max Werner's gook wagon. The twin exhaust pipes served a real purpose by cutting down on back pressure, which was further decreased by the special straight-through mufflers Dave had purchased from a speed parts house and installed in the exhausts. So when the Model A backed off its pipes Dave listened happily.

Normally the straight-through mufflers were fine but right now even their comparatively light check on exhaust noise was going to be eliminated. For as the Model A coasted swiftly down the hill Dave's right hand moved toward the cut-out lever under the dashboard. At the bottom of the hill glowed the gas pumps of Chet Coley's filling station. Inside the station would be Constable Currie drinking birch beer and chewing the fat with Chet Coley.

Under his goggles Dave smiled grimly as he thought of the effect the cut-out would have on Constable Currie; that bottle of birch beer might be blasted right out of the constable's startled hand. Gosh, poor old Constable Currie. With a grunt of pity punctuated by the staccato coughing of the tail pipes Dave turned the cut-out lever and stepped on the gas.

Bbbrrraaattt. What a raucous, ear-splitting, wonderful noise! For now the roar of the Model A was not even modified by its straight-through mufflers but was hurled with its full volume of noisy belligerence upon the peace and quiet of the countryside; not to mention the unsuspecting eardrums of Constable Currie.

Constable Currie was supposed to have radar ears for the challenging noises of hot rods. From miles away the sound of a "souped up" car was said to register acutely on eardrums that were deaf to the barking of dogs or the chirping of crickets. If this were so, then a hot rod with its cut-out open should make the constable's sensitive eardrums vibrate with excitement.

As he blasted by the filling station Dave was thrilled by the daring prank he had perpetrated. He hoped it would pin back the ears of those members of the Milltown Hot Rod Club who were listening in their hiding places on the back roads. It would awe them, that shattering noise; it would raucously remind them that a candidate for membership was undergoing an initation which none of the members, safe in their hiding places, had been made to do.

Satisfied by the loud blast of defiance, Dave steered his pride and joy up the hill beyond the station, then slowed his speed and silenced the cut-out. It had served its purpose; Santa Claus was undoubtedly aroused and hurrying to his constable's car hidden behind the filling station, his radar ears tuned to the cutout's tantalizing racket. Now let the object of that tuning fade, to lend an air of mystery and suspense to the Constable's provocation.

Chuckling to himself Dave could almost hear the constable cursing, "That hot rod! Just as I'm locatin' him he goes back on his mufflers. But I'll get him jess the same. I'm not gonna let a hot rodder make a fool out of me. No sirree Bob!"

And the constable would jump into his car, slam the door and dash out of his hiding place, siren wailing, red light flashing. Or would he play possum, siren off, red light out, until just before the arrest?

Arrest—Phooey! Dave snorted with scorn and once more tromped the gas pedal. The Model A answered with a thrilling burst of speed along the straight flat road that traversed the ridge Dave had reached. And riding proudly with that speed Dave told himself that no constable's car could possibly catch a souped up Model A.

Chapter VII

THE road along the top of the ridge ran past Irv Lockwood's farm and the cider mill. Then it roller-coasted
with dips and rises before plunging down Dead Man's
Hill. This hill was a steep descent broken by an S
curve blasted out of solid rock. On the upstretch would
be a fine piece of road for experimental driving and it
was a shame, in a way, Dave thought, that Constable
Currie patroled it so conscientiously. The rock-bound
S turn was an exciting challenge and the long straight
run at the top of the ridge provided a perfect home
stretch. It was just the kind of hill climb a hot rod
needed to test its speed and its ability to hold the road.
For anything more than a slight slip on either curve of
the S turn could smash the car against a crude un-

yielding fence of spike-shaped boulders. If an errant car hurdled this obstacle it would plunged over a precipice down to a rocky stream bed.

The dangers of Dead Man's Hill were well indicated. As Dave's hot rod left the straight flatness of the ridge road his headlights picked up three highway signs in luminous paint. He knew them by heart. The first one said SLIPPERY WHEN WET; the second, STEEP HILL—TRUCKS DESCEND IN GEAR; the third was just a big black S against a field of orange paint.

Dave ignored the warnings. They were meant for the driver who couldn't tell the difference between a carburetor and a supercharger. Drivers like that didn't care what was under the hood; they had no love for motors and were baffled and irritated when their abused engines burned bearings or simply refused to start. It was for such ignoramuses that the state traffic commission put up all those fancy signs and strung necklaces of reflectors around the loops of the S curve. Gosh, how many driving aids did those creeps need?

Putta-putt-putt-pock-pock. The Model A proudly backed off its pipes as Dave coasted down Dead Man's Hill. Alternately braking or gunning his engine Dave gave his hot rod just enough speed to make the tires sob gently around the S-turn curves. It was a satisfying sound, that gentle sobbing of the tires. Dave was smiling as he came out of the S and accelerated across a crest before coasting down a steep short stretch to a small stone bridge.

The time for the test was at hand. Suddenly Dave had an idea that acted on his pulse like foot pressure on a gas pedal: Dead Man's Hill with its steep S turn and its ridge road could be much more than just a challenge ground for a contest with a constable. Suppose a mile were measured up through the S turn and along the ridge? Then he, Dave Neil, could set a record for the run that other hot rodders could shoot at, including that swaggering braggart Max Werner. It would be something like that race up Pike's Peak that Dave had once seen in a newsreel. He could almost hear the announcers voice over the public address system: "And here is a new record for the course, folks, set by Dave Neil of Milltown—one minute and umpteen seconds!"

What would Max Werner and the Milltown hot rodders think of that! Dave smiled as he imagined the awed, admiring faces. Fame at last. Dave Neil, hero. Not only the hot rod driver who had successfully challenged Constable Currie but the driver who had established a record for the mile run up Dead Man's Hill.

Dave was so pleased with the exciting prospects of the new plan that he hardly noticed he had crossed the stone bridge and approached the cluster of buildings that marked the center of Branchville: the town hall, the Congregational church, the neat stores of the

67

new shopping center. But he did notice a couple of kids on bikes. As he passed them he gunned his engine and was pleased to see them point and stare at the racy lines of the Model A. Then he drove proudly around the shopping center, revving up his engine with raucous bursts of power. He wished the two kids on the bikes knew what he was going to do—they'd be impressed. He really should have an audience for his forthcoming feat. But there was hardly anyone in sight; all the stores were closed. Branchville was as dead as a door nail.

Except for one thing—the filling station. That was open and brightly illuminated. Dave didn't need any gas but he slowed down. For purring beside the pumps, as sleek and powerful as a panther, stood a long, low, red and black phaeton. Its hood was up, the longest hood Dave had ever seen. And staring at the power plant under the hood with eyes trained for mechanical features Dave spotted 1-2-3-4 carburetors. Four carburetors! Jumping catfish! Dave's foot came off the accelerator and reached for the brake. Here was a car that should be studied. Four carburetors, a quad job as they said at the hot rod club.

A quad job Dave repeated in an awed whisper. How many carbs does my rod have? Just one. Jeepers. Twin pipes but only one carburetor. I've got to get another carburetor. Imagine owning a car with a "quad job."

Think of the acceleration you could get up Dead Man's Hill!

Ka-pomph. The Model A coughed a jealous protest and stalled. In his admiration of the sleek phaeton Dave had neglected his clutch. But perhaps no one had noticed it. Yes they had—he had—the driver of the phaeton, a big man who suddenly straightened up and towered over the huge car's hood. He must have sharp mechanical ears, thought Dave, although he looks more like a college fullback. A blond, close-cropped head sat squarely on shoulders that seemed about to burst out of a bright red sweater. The broad face over the sweater was watching the stalled Model A with a look of mild interest and perhaps, thought Dave, slight contempt. That look increased Dave's annoyance with himself. This was a heck of a time to stall a car, in front of a phaeton with four carburetors. Irritably Dave pushed the starter button, stepped on the accelerator. Ah, there was the good brash roar again. Shifting into first, revving up the engine, Dave peeled rubber and screeched out of the filling station like a hyena escaping from its cage. And as he raced away, belittling thoughts raced with him about the phaeton's driver. A rich playboy probably, with money to burn. A car like that would cost several thousand bucks. So phooey on the phaeton.

Gunning his motor Dave headed for the stone bridge which marked the foot of Dead Man's Hill. He would show that playboy with the phaeton; he'd show Constable Currie; he'd show Max Werner and the hot rodders.

Dave raced his Model A across the bridge, roared up the hill. He was so excited and indignant that he almost forgot about the timed hill climb. Almost. He remembered as he crossed the crest before the S turn. Hitting his brakes he swung the Model A into a convenient driveway on the right, noticing the sign that marked it: Dr. J. D. Brown, Veterinarian. "Thanks for the turn-around Doc," said Dave and drove back down the hill.

Once more at the stone bridge he turned the Model A with a neat maneuver, came to a dead stop, and reached for the flashlight clipped to the dashboard. Unfortunately the second hand on his wrist watch was not phosphorescent; that would make the timing difficult. But he could get it reasonably accurate by giving himself a ten-second leeway, counting the seconds out loud as he put the flashlight away and revved up the engine. He noticed that when the minute hand was exactly on the minute mark, the second hand was at 40. So at 30 on the second hand and two minutes to nine on the minute hand, he would start his count.

"1-2-3-4." The flashlight was clipped back on the dashboard.

"5-6-7-8." The engine was revved up.

"9-10." Peel rubber!

70

The Model A leaped forward, tires screeching. Shifting into second Dave sent his hot rod racing up the hill toward the S turn. The engine roared belligerently, the tires whined their complaint. Dave's heart was pumping like a piston as he reached the first crest, double clutched, shifted into high.

Hunched over the wheel, Dave leaned into the hill as the Model A raced past the vet's driveway and hurtled up into dangerous territory, into the S turn with the shelf of solid rock on one side, the stern stone fence and precipice on the other. His foot throbbing on the accelerator, his hands gripping the wheel, Dave's whole body tingled with the excitement of his speed and the challenge of the curve.

Without warning he found himself in a sickening skid. The car's front wheels were turned to the right to take the curve but the rear wheels were sliding in the opposite direction. It was a horrible feeling. Dave's breath choked off, his heart seemed suddenly to be beating in his throat. And the pretty necklace of glass reflectors strung along the stone fence became the glistening jaws of a monster that would swallow the Model A and its driver.

For a fateful second or two Dave was frozen with fear. In that brief time his mind seemed paralyzed but his body worked automatically. He jerked his foot off the accelerator, slammed on the brake. The skid worsened with the tires screaming as if in a death grip.

Suddenly from somewhere, out of all he had ever read and heard about high-speed driving, came a phrase of warning "Steer into the skid! Steer into the skid!" But it seemed like the worst thing to do. He had to overcome a powerful urge to keep the front wheels turned in the opposite direction.

It seemed to take hours. Actually it took seconds, flying skidding seconds. Somehow Dave succeeded in steering into the skid and at the same time he released his brake. The effect was felt almost at once. The Model A's tail slowed its spin so that its collision with the stone fence was just a minor bang. And by gunning the motor and shifting quickly Dave was able to drive his car out of serious trouble and keep it climbing the hill toward the inside curve of the S turn.

His breath came back, his heart returned to its proper position, though still pounding like a piston. Fear faded and excitement once more took its place as Dave double-clutched, shifted into high and steered the Model A up toward the steeper, safer inside curve. The skid had been frightening but it had also been thrilling. If only Max Werner and the Milltown hot rodders could have seen that skid and the way it was mastered.

Thinking of Max made Dave glance upward to the left. His search swept over a rocky gorge through a thin grove of hemlocks to the top of the hill. Where was that signal Max was supposed to flash? There it was, shining down through the trees—one long flash. Dave shivered and decoded: Constable Currie had moved out of the filling station and had set his speed trap at Hurlbutt's cider mill near the top of the hill. That was fine. Santa Claus would get a real run for his money.

Grinning nervously under his goggles Dave gave himself a pep talk: Poor old Santa Claus was going to look like a fool chasing a hot rod that had just established a record for a hill climb through an S curve. Talk about killing two birds with one stone! Dave laughed out loud as he roared around the S curve's second loop.

His driving wasn't quite so foolhardy this time; his foot was light on the accelerator as he neared the shelf of sheer rock—if he ever smacked into that unyielding wall it would be goodnight Model A and driver. He cornered more carefully. But he skidded just the same, a slight but satisfying slide, a soft skid. He recovered nicely from it by double-clutching, shifting down to second, accelerating.

Ah, that felt good, gunning the engine out of that skid. He roared up to the top of the hill with the cool air rushing past his intoxicated head: watch out, Santa Claus. I'm not only going to make you eat my dust but in doing it I'm going to set a record that other hot rods will envy.

As the Model A reached the top of the hill Dave

double-clutched, shifted into high again, then flipped the cut-out lever. *Bbbrrraaattt*. The brash noise of the Model A became a deafening roar. In Dave's ears it was a wild, wonderful song, the perfect music to accompany his bid for leadership, his challenge to Constable Currie, and his record-setting hill climb. The last named was perhaps the most glorious of all three objectives but all three added up to the biggest thrill Dave had ever experienced.

With the air rushing, the cut-out blasting, Dave was almost delirious with delight. But he did not forget the location of the speed trap. As he roared past the cider mill he glanced to his right and saw two parking lights flash brightly into headlights. The Constable's car! Dave's grip tightened on the wheel, his jaw clenched as he listened anxiously for the revved up engine, the whine of the siren. He didn't hear them. They were drowned out by the defiant roar of the Model A's cut-out. Dave's reflex of fear vanished before a defiant laugh, an exultant cry, "Come on, Santa Claus, see if you can climb down my chimney. Ten to one you get stuck!"

As if in answer to this challenge two disks of light suddenly glowed in the Model A's rear-vision mirror. Again Dave felt a twinge of fear. But the glow of the disks did not brighten; the constable was not gaining. Dave's fear faded as his exultation rushed back with the night air and the roar of the cut-out.

74

Confident now, Dave turned his thoughts to the timing of the run that had measured almost a mile on the speedometer. He was roaring along the flat straight road on top of the ridge bearing down on the second intersection, Irv Lockwood's farmhouse. As he blasted by the screen of hemlocks he marked it on his speedometer—just two-tenths short of a mile. And he noted something else too, a flickering of lights from behind the screen of trees; the Milltown hot rodders were signaling from their hiding places. Those lights gave Dave a glow of satisfaction; the hot rodders were in a perfect position to see the complete defeat of Constable Currie.

One-tenth—two-tenths. The mile! Dave glanced anxiously at the phosphorescent hands of his wrist watch. Over two minutes. Gosh that seemed slow. Disappointment stabbed him as he eased up on the accelerator and started counting seconds, "2-3-4." He reached for the flashlight clipped to the dashboard, then glanced quickly in the rear-vision mirror to check the constable. No sign of him—outclassed—outdistanced.

"5-6-7." A ray of light illuminated the second hand on Dave's wrist watch. Two minutes and seven seconds. Not so hot. He shook his head in disappointment. Then he consoled himself. It wasn't too bad considering the steep grade, the S turn, the fact that the run was made at night. Of course Max Werner would scoff at that time. But just let him beat it with his hot rod, not his motorcycle.

Dave gunned the engine again to be sure that the constable was left far behind, then eased up for the hill ahead. By the time he passed Chet Coley's filling station he was down to a comfortable speed and the cut-out was turned off. There was no need for further defiance of the laws of Branchville. They had been badly broken; Constable Currie had been humiliated; Dave had passed his initiation, and a hill climb record set which could probably withstand all the assaults it would suffer from the hot rod club.

Happier than he had ever been in his seventeen years of life, Dave drove his Model A across the town line and on toward the hot rod club where the group had agreed to meet. What fun that meeting would be, with the members all gathered around, awed and admiring. For the first time in my life, thought Dave, I'll be a hero to the gang. And what has made it all possible? This wonderful car, this marvelous Model A. On an impulse springing from his gratitude, Dave reached out toward the car that had performed so well and patted it affectionately on the cowl as if it were a magnificently trained animal that had just brought its master a blue ribbon.

Chapter VIII

As HE drove back to the hot rod club that warm spring night, Dave felt like a mountaineer who had scaled a dangerous peak: he looks down, catches his breath, and says, "Whew! Where did I ever get the nerve to do it!" Then comes the recognition of the daring deed and finally the award—in this case membership in the Milltown Hot Rod Club.

The award was heralded by the sharp staccato sound of an approaching motorcycle. The noise sent a shiver down Dave's back as he hurried to the club house window and stared at the swiftly approaching single headlight. Max was the first one to return, obviously.

Bbbrrraaattt. There was a fierce final blast from the Harley-Davidson and a sudden silence as Max cut off his engine and dismounted. Quickly Dave backed away from the window, picked up a magazine, feigned interest. He would be casual, nonchalant, "Oh, hello, Max, what kept you? I thought you might have been pinched by Santa Claus." Better not rub it in too badly. Max would probably be jealous; he might be dejected, humble.

Max was neither dejected nor humble. He swaggered into the club as loud and self-assured as ever. And his voice was scornful, "That was a flop, Dave, nice try but a flop."

A flop? For a moment Dave stared, incredulous.

Then he bridled. "Listen Max, you don't seem to realize what I did. I not only made a monkey out of Constable Currie—"

"You did not!" Max broke in belligerently. He pushed his peaked cap back on his head, hooked his thumbs into his glittering belt.

"Wha' d' y' mean, I did not?" Dave's voice tried to blunt with indignation a disturbing needle of doubt.

"You just didn't, Dave," said Max smiling with sly sympathy. "Sure you outraced Santa Claus but any kid on a bike could have done it."

"Oh yeah?" Dave sputtered. "Listen Max, I don't care what you say, my Model A outraced the constable's car because that hot rod of mine is the—"

Max broke in again, "Your heap outraced the constable's car because his jalopy broke down."

"Broke down?" Dave stared, open mouthed.

"Yeah, broke down." Max spat out the words. "And what kind of a two-car race is it if one of the cars breaks down?"

Dave was trying to think of an answer when a discordant symphony of squealing brakes and racing engines based on the raucous rhythmic banging of car doors, announced the arrival of the other members of the hot rod club.

As they trooped in, Dave anxiously studied their faces. He found some new respect—the Model A had made an impression. But the respectful looks hesitated just for a second or so and then swept on to the sharp figure of Max. And Dave, his mouth dry, his fists partly clenched, found himself listening against his will as Max said, "I was just tellin' Dave here what happened to Santa Claus, how his jalopy gave up."

"That wasn't my fault!" Dave blurted out. "Can I help it if the constable's car breaks down?"

" 'Course you can't, Dave," said Max. His sharp voice seemed to soften. "But I still say what I said to you before the fellas came in—that if one car breaks down in a two-car race it's no contest. Right, fellas?" Max appealed to his hand-picked jury.

"Right, Max." They all obediently nodded their heads.

Dave watched, disheartened. He swallowed hard. Why did Constable Currie's car have to break down

79

just at the wrong time and ruin the race? Why did it break down anyway? Irritably Dave voiced the second question.

Max gave an impatient shrug to his shoulders. "How should I know?"

But Ronnie Felton spoke up, delighted to contribute something to the discussion. "I think Santa Claus blew a gasket," he said.

"Blew a gasket?" Max snorted contemptuously. "That's what you always think happens."

"Well it does happen a lot, doesn't it, Dave?" said Ronnie defensively.

"It could be a number of things," Dave said, confident of his superior knowledge of engines. "It might be a fuel lock, clogged carburetor, fouled plugs." He smiled sourly, "You're sure it wasn't a flat tire?"

Ronnie didn't realize he was being kidded. "Oh, I'm sure it wasn't a flat tire. 'Cause as soon as I saw Santa Claus couldn't chase me I came out on the highway, cruised real close and gave him the bird."

"Oh my, weren't we daring?" said Max in a mockingly high voice.

Ronnie's face flushed. His voice took on a touch of defiance. "Well, maybe I was. Santa Claus wasn't exactly helpless. Someone had come to his rescue. And boy, what a heap that rescuer had."

"Yeah, I saw it," said Max superciliously, "A Stutz Bearcat."

For a moment Dave forgot his chagrin. "A Stutz Bearcat? Was it a phaeton with four carburetors?"

Max scowled. "How the heck should I know? Expect me to see under the hood? Wha'd'y' think I got—X-ray eyes?"

This brought a laugh from the hot rodders but Dave persisted defiantly, "If it's the same car I saw at the filling station in Branchville it's not a Stutz Bearcat and it does have four carburetors."

"Not a Stutz Bearcat?" Max sneered his dissent. "Listen, don't yuh think I can recognize a Stutz Bearcat when I see one?"

"Sure yuh can, Max," said Ronnie Felton.

Dave glared at Ronnie. Now there was a real stooge. The more Max slapped him down the better Ronnie liked it. Was I ever that way? Dave asked himself. Gosh, perhaps I was. Never again. I've got my own hot rod now, the best in the club, and I put on a swell show tonight no matter what Max says. He thinks he knows it all. Jeepers, I've forgotten more about cars than he's ever learned.

Max was delivering a lecture on the fine points of Stutz Bearcats. Dave interrupted, "I still don't think that car is a Stutz."

Max scowled, "Who cares what you think?" He lit a cigarette, blew a stream of smoke at Dave.

Taunted beyond endurance, Dave blurted out, "I'll bet you a buck it wasn't a Stutz Bearcat!"

81

"O.K.," said Max, smiling sardonically. He winked at his faithful followers. "You're witness to that bet, fellas."

"And another one besides!" cried Dave, swept away on a tide of defiance, "that your heap can't beat the record my Model A made on Dead Man's Hill!"

"O.K. kid," said Max, "whatever your record was, my V-8'll beat it. Bear witness, fellas."

The hot rodders nodded like a jury spellbound by an eloquent lawyer.

Max took another drag from his cigarette, "O.K. Dave, the bets are placed. Your dough's as good as gone but bets or no bets you're still evadin' the issue."

"What issue?" said Dave hotly. He fumbled nervously in his pocket, pulled out a cigarette, lit it, inhaled. *Wham.* The warm smoke struck his chest like a blow to the solar plexus. He gasped for air, coughed until tears ran down his cheeks.

Max led the laughter, then slapped Dave stoutly on the back. "Take it easy, kid, the pulmotor will get here any minute now."

Delighted with his own wit, Max tipped his head back and roared with laughter. The others followed suit.

Dave fought for breath, found it, furiously voiced the question again, "What issue am I evading? Come on, tell me."

"Relax, Dave, relax," said Max infuriatingly. He

smugly inhaled smoke, blew it out smoothly. "Listen, Dave, this is the issue. You didn't outrace Constable Currie—you didn't spring his speed trap. His car broke down. But the way you've been talking and actin' around here anyone'd think you'd run Santa Claus right off the road. Right, fellas?"

The hot rodders nodded obediently.

"Well, Dave," Max continued confidently, "the way I've got it figured you either gotta do it all over again or chicken out."

"Chicken." Dave threw his cigarette on the floor, ground it out. How he detested that word "chicken." It seemed to sum up all of Max's approach to problems. "Chicken." Max would drive his hot rod through traffic at breakneck speed, weaving, cutting in and out, passing cars on the right, with speed, tension, and fear mounting until someone screamed "Chicken, Max, chicken!" and then Max would slow down with a derisively triumphant laugh that steered scorn on the frightened "chicken."

"Chicken." It was a terrible term. It twisted facts, pinned the label of cowardice on people who were simply being sensible. "Listen," cried Dave, "I don't care what you say, I did what I said I'd do. It wasn't my fault that the constable's car broke down. Why should I stick my neck out again? I'm not chicken and you all know it."

"'Course we all know it, Dave," said Max with a

hearty slap on Dave's back. "Nobody called you chicken. Don't get me wrong, kid. But still you gotta admit you didn't outrace the constable. How could you? He wasn't even in the race. So in my humble opinion, Dave"—Max flicked the ash off his cigarette —"you gotta do it all over again. Am I right, fellas?"

Max smiled winningly at his followers and was immediately rewarded by a vote of confidence.

Dave was seething. But he said nothing—he was incapable of speech. He just stood there glaring, his clenched fists hidden in his pockets. One of them found his pack of cigarettes, clutched it, mashed its contents into a mess of tobacco shreds. He'd never smoke again, never. He had only started it because it was the smart thing to do—because Max the leader smoked and the sheep followed their leader. Well, he was through following the leader—being a sheep— to heck with the club! But he'd show these guys once and for all that he wasn't chicken; he'd race Constable Currie once more and prove to himself and the blind, faithful followers of Max Werner that a hot rod club deserved something better than a president who performed his daring deeds on a motorcycle.

Chapter IX

POOR old Santa Claus. There he stood at the side of the road shining the beams of a flashlight over the broad shoulders of Webb Walden.

"Can't understand it," complained Constable Currie. "She was goin' along fine and then suddenly she gets a terrible fit of coughin' and collapses. And me just closin' in on that hot rodder."

Webb Walden turned and looked over the flashlight beam at the constable's shadowy outline, the fuzzy blur of the constable's whiskers, the faint glint of the badge.

Webb smiled. His voice was deep, slow, calm. "You were just about to make the pinch, ay, Constable?"

"That's right," said Constable Currie. "I had my

speed trap all set 'cause I knew who was comin'—he sure advertised it with that cut-out of his. Why, Webb, the use of that cut-out alone is a violation of the rules of the road punishable by a fifty-dollar fine."

He began to crackle with excitement. "There are two places where I set my speed traps, at the cider mill and at Irv Lockwood's farm. This time I used the cider mill 'cause it's nearer the crest of the hill and I figured I'd catch that hot rodder 'fore he could hit his top speed. Pretty coony, ay, Webb?"

"Very," said Webb. He turned his big broad head into the flashlight's beam. "Looks like you got some dirt in your gas; your jets are clogged, Constable."

"What say?" said Constable Currie, peering into the engine. "Jets? Don't tell me that engine is jet propelled. It sure didn't act like it a few minutes ago." Constable Currie cackled at his own wit.

Webb Walden straightened up. "No, I don't mean jets as in jet propulsion. The jets in your carburetor are very fine openings 40/1000ths of an inch in diameter."

"Land sakes!" exclaimed Constable Currie.

"The gas is drawn through those tiny openings," said Webb Walden, "but if the jets get clogged your engine doesn't get any gas."

The constable clucked his tongue. "Well, well, that's mighty int'restin', Webb. I swear I always did mean to learn more about engines but I never did get around to it."

Webb nodded and smiled. "That's not the first time I've heard that, Constable. I'd say ninety out of a hundred drivers in the United States never look under the hood, and of the remaining ten, nine just check for oil and water."

"Mebbe so," said Constable Currie; and then, as Webb Walden once more leaned over the engine, the Constable resumed his description of his race against the hot rodder. "There I was settin' in my speed trap, engine runnin' real nice. Suddenly I hear that hot rodder comin' up Dead Man's Hill goin' lickety split." The Constable's voice started shaking with excitement; so did the flashlight's beam.

"Could you steady that light, please?" asked Webb Walden without turning.

Constable Currie managed to steady the light but his voice continued to vibrate. "I shifted gears, stepped on the gas and swung out right behind that racin' fool." The cackle was high now and thin. "He was goin' like a bat out of Hades, Webb, but I pushed my accelerator right down to the floor and started after him. I was gainin' on him too, but by gum, just as I was about to make the pinch—"

"Your float valve stuck," said Webb Walden calmly.

"Ay?" Constable Currie squeaked off as if brakes had suddenly been applied.

"The float valve," Webb repeated, standing up, towering over the constable. "It works like a float valve in the toilet."

"Well, bless my britches," said Constable Currie; and he brushed his whiskers instead. "There sure is more to an engine than meets the eye."

"Sure is," said Webb smiling. "Here's how it works, Constable. The gas flows into the float bowl and pushes up the hollow brass float. When that float reaches a specific height it closes the float valve. Then as the gas is burned the hollow float sinks, opening the float valve. That's the way your float valve was operating until some dirt got in there and gummed up the works. Your float valve got stuck—open."

"Land o' goshen!" said Constable Currie in disgust. "Clogged jets, stuck float valves. Had no idea a carburetor could be so complicated."

Webb laughed. "But it can be. Carburetor trouble has lost plenty of hill climbs and road races."

"Hill climbs, road races?" The Constable's tone was disapproving. "Sounds illegal to me, Webb. None of that around here."

Webb's tone was light. "Well, Constable, would you rather have it illegal, dangerous, and a nuisance, or legal, supervised, and reasonably safe—besides being fun for a lot of people?"

"Don't see how it could be either fun or reasonably safe," said Constable Currie. "And I'm mighty sure it'll be illegal as long as I'm the constable of this township. Can't have any shenanigans like that in my territory. No sir."

"Can't have 'em?" said Webb Walden under his breath, "Constable, you've already got 'em."

"Ay?" said Constable Currie, cupping his free hand to one ear. "What say?"

"I said if you'll move that flashlight a little more this way I'll clean up this carburetor for you. Incidentally, don't you think a constable's car should have a little more power than this one?"

"How d'y' mean, more power?"

"Well," said Webb slowly, "I could put in another carburetor and give the engine a high-compression head. Let me soup up your car, Constable, and you won't have so much trouble running down these hot rodders."

"Hmm," Constable Currie combed his whiskers, "Soup it up, ay? Don't know exactly what that means but if it means catchin' hot rodders then I'm for it. Yes sir."

As Webb Walden cleaned the constable's carburetor he arranged private thoughts about the law, road racing, and hill climbs. Dead Man's Hill with its S turn would be "a natural" for a legally supervised hill climb. It wouldn't have to be an official Sports Car Club hill climb like the one at Equinox, Vermont, or

Wilkes-Barre, Pennsylvania; but it would serve the purpose—to introduce controlled speed to the community; to show the townspeople and the authorities that under proper auspices hill climbing and road racing could be constructive sports.

Constable Currie had expressed disapproval of hill climbs and road races; little wonder with the merciless hot rodders making a monkey out of him. But with two carburetors and a high compression head the constable's car could catch those irritating hot rodders. And those dangerous driving, law-breaking show-offs should be apprehended.

If I help poor old Constable Currie do his duty, Webb Walden told himself, perhaps he'll cooperate with me on a legal hill climb.

Chapter X

DAVE was worried. His hands trembled as he cleaned the Model A's spark plugs, adjusted the carburetor. He listened questioningly as he pressed the starter button. The Model A roared its loud brash answer. It was a wonderful noise but somehow it lacked its old reassurance. It didn't give Dave the confidence he wanted, the confidence he had felt in his first challenge of Constable Currie. Because this time he was definitely doing something he didn't want to do. And he knew that he had let himself be maneuvered into it by Max Werner.

Switching on his headlights, he shifted into first and drove the Model A out of the barn. His mother called to him out the kitchen window as he moved down the

91

dirt driveway, "Be careful, Dave. And don't stay out too late. It's a school night, you know."

He knew. He also knew that he had lied to her about where he was going and what he intended to do. His mother's voice irritated him and he knew why. It was a call of conscience and he was ignoring it against his better judgment. He was suddenly angry at himself as well as at the world.

To show his defiance he gave the wheel a wrench that spun the Model A out on the road. Shifting sharply, he tromped the accelerator and peeled rubber. There was an exciting scream as his back tires clawed frantically at the macadam, then they gripped the surface and sent the Model A rocketing down the road.

He felt a little better. And the atmosphere of the hot rod club helped. Once more the hot rodders had respect and admiration in their looks and voices. They admired Dave's daring; he was a good sport to try again. Even Max said so, placing a friendly hand on Dave's shoulder, "I'll cooperate with yuh just like last time; I'll go right down the line with yuh, Dave boy."

Oh sure, said Dave to himself, right down the line— right down the back roads—while I'm out on the highway risking my neck, my driver's license, and my savings account. Aloud Dave said, "Listen Max, no matter what happens to the constable's car this time, this race counts. Right?"

"Of course, Dave," said Max smoothly. "This one is

for sure, breakdown or no breakdown. You betcha. And incidentally Dave, speakin' of bets, they're still on, eh? Two bucks. My money says that the guy who helped Constable Currie was drivin' a Stutz Bearcat. My second buck says that my heap can make faster time up Dead Man's Hill."

"O.K." Dave managed to keep his voice steady in spite of a dry tongue and an uneasy puckering in the back of his mouth.

Max grinned. "Now just to keep everything on the up-and-up, Dave, I brought along a couple of stop watches so that we can get the real accurate time for your run up the hill." Proudly Max produced the stop watches, showed them to the awed audience.

Dave stared at the stop watches. Why didn't I think of that? Dave asked himself. But there were so many other things to think about—adjusting the carburetor, cleaning spark plugs, testing tires, tightening brakes. Who would think of anything as fancy as a stop watch? Why Max, of course. Listen to him now. He was like an air force squadron commander briefing his men before an attack.

Traveling on back roads, Max would meet Dave at the stone bridge a few minutes before nine o'clock. The hill climb would start at exactly nine. Max would check the timing at the stone bridge with one stop watch. Ronnie Felton would do the timing at the end of the measured mile.

"So the time will be double checked for accuracy, Dave," Max concluded, pleased by his own planning.

Once again the Model A soothed Dave's irritation and restored his confidence. The noise of its engine sang sweetly in his ears, the night air rushed excitingly over his head, and the gas pedal provided a thrilling contact with the engine he had assembled. It was wonderful the way that pedal responded to the slightest pressure. Push it down now smoothly but firmly for this hill. Feel it answer faithfully, immediately; listen to the engine's confident roar—right up the hill in high without pressing the pedal against the floor. That's power for you, power you created by hard work and mechanical ability, exciting power, thrilling speed, more speed than any other hot rod in the club.

The Model A soared over the top of the hill and Dave's headlights again picked up the significant sign: "BRANCHVILLE. Incorporated 1825. TOWN LINE." Enemy territory patrolled by Constable Currie. Phooey on Constable Currie; his car couldn't catch a caterpillar. Dave laughed defiantly as he steered with his left hand and with his right reached for the cut-out lever. Poor old Santa Claus. He'd be in Chet Coley's filling station as usual, drinking birch beer. The sound of the cut-out would blow that beer into the constable's beard.

Bbbrrraaattt. The brash noise of the Model A, released from the restraints of the muffler, blasted over

94

the quiet countryside. It was an exciting ear-splitting sound. The roar of the cut-out, the thrill of the fast drive produced in Dave an intoxication that obliterated all twinges of conscience about the lie to his mother, the flagrant illegality of this high-speed challenge of the constable. The Model A roared by the illuminated gas pumps of Chet Coley's filling station and Dave soared through a world of his own, an intoxicating world of speed and power created by his own hands and controlled by the pressure of his foot on the gas pedal, the touch of his hands on the wheel.

On he roared past the filling station, with the cool air rushing over the windscreen to meet him, searching swiftly but vainly for an opening around his goggles, brushing over the mouth stretched in a thin tense line, then whistling past his ears.

Up the hill he roared and on to the long straight level stretch atop the ridge where Constable Currie baited his speed traps. As he tightened his grip on the wheel Dave increased the pressure on the gas pedal. The Model A spurted, blasted by one trap, then another; they had not been set. Dave's first surmise had been correct—Constable Currie was in Chet Coley's filling station. He would now be hustling to his car, birch beer dripping from his whiskers. Poor old Santa Claus. A pathetic kind of guy.

Dave eased up on the accelerator, flipped the cut-out lever to its normal position, and smoothly steered the Model A down Dead Man's Hill. With the cut-out off, the comparative quiet was broken only by the muttering of the Model A backing off its pipes.

As the hot rod's headlights picked up the stone bridge at the foot of the hill Dave glanced at his wrist watch. It was closer to nine than he had realized so he decided against a tour of Branchville's shopping center. Fanning his brakes, he slowed the Model A, turned it around, maneuvered it into a starting position facing the hill he had just descended. Then he turned off his engine, switched to his parking lights, pushed his goggles back on his head, and impatiently asked, "Where is Max, the great leader?"

"Hi Dave." The answer was sudden, startling as Max stepped out of the darkness, the reflectors on his motorcycle belt flickering in the glow of the Model A's parking lights. Again Dave fearfully noticed that disturbing resemblance to a motorcycle cop about to make an arrest. But Max wasn't a cop, he was a schemer, a planner, a cooperative pusher in a risky adventure. Too cooperative, thought Dave, and taking too little of the risk.

"I heard you blast Santa Claus with yuh cut-out, Dave." Max leaned on the Model A and grinned into the cockpit. "Nice work, kid. You're a credit to the club."

Dave grunted. Max was not only too arrogant and domineering—he was corny. Dave glanced at his wrist watch. "About time to get going," he said. He found himself suddenly impatient to get started, to get away from Max Werner. Dave didn't even like the possessive way in which Max leaned on the Model A. And what was he prattling about?

"I tooled around Branchville," said Max with a swagger in his voice. "Dead town. Humph. I woke it up a little. By the way, I ran into that rich snob Webb Walden and his Stutz Bearcat."

"Huh?" Dave pricked up his ears. Webb Walden and his Stutz Bearcat? It was just like Max Werner to snoop around and find out that guy's name—Webb Walden. Max always made a point of knowing who was doing what and when. But Max didn't know much about the most important subject of all, automobiles. That car was not a Stutz Bearcat. But what the devil was it?

Max was talking on. "Listen Dave, somethin' fishy is cookin'; I hear this Webb Walden is a super-duper mechanic and I think he's in cahoots with Constable Currie."

"How come?" Dave was startled for the second time in as many minutes.

"Just got a hunch." Max straightened up, pulled out a stop watch, set it. "Walden fixed the constable's car, didn't he? Why should he do that? Just for the love of engines? Naaa. He's got something cookin', that guy has."

97

"Well, so what?" said Dave sharply. "What's he going t' do, chase me in his sports car? What good would it do him?"

"No good," said Max. His voice dropped its swagger, assumed an insinuating tone. "But suppose Webb Walden is in cahoots with the constable; suppose Walden souped up the constable's car? That might be sort of, uh, embarrassin' Dave; might make a much closer race of it tonight."

"Might at that," said Dave, trying to keep his tone indifferent. He could feel his hands get sweaty as his mouth got dry.

Max pretended to be studying the stop watch. "It's not too late to back out, Dave."

"And be called chicken!" Dave snapped out the sentence.

"Why, Dave," Max looked up from the watch, his face full of feigned surprise. "No one's ever called you chicken."

"Right," said Dave hoarsely, "and they're not going to either. Now set that watch, Max, and give me the signal. I'm going to give you a real record to shoot at."

"O.K., Dave, O.K.; don't get excited." Max's tone was mockingly soothing. "Tell yuh what I'm gonna do, Dave. I'm gonna hold up my right hand with the handkerchief in it. That'll be like the starter's flag, see? Now you rev up your engine and when I yell go and drop the flag you peel rubber and wind it out. O.K.?"

Dave nodded. He didn't trust his tongue; this was no time to start an argument. So Dave kept quiet. But he seethed inside. He was nervous about the hill climb and the challenge to Constable Currie; he was worried for fear that Webb Walden had souped up the constable's car. And he was irritated by Max's confident use of esoteric terms like "drop the flag," "rev it up," "peel rubber," "wind it out." If Max were such a hot shot why had he burned out the bearings on his V-8? Max was just a blustery bag of wind.

Annoyed and worried, Dave turned to the Model A and asked for reassurance. He got it. The engine caught, roared. Ah, there was a real friend, the best friend of all, the engine he had created. His left foot pressing the clutch pedal to the floor, Dave's right hand carefully moved the gear shift into first. Clutch still in he revved up the engine. Its brash noise rose and fell, *arroom-rroom.* Glancing up, Dave saw Max's right hand raise the white handkerchief. He heard Max's voice, harsh, challenging, "Ready?"

Dave's lips were tight with tension, a tension that froze his face, moistened his hands, and sent unsettling flickers of nausea down to his cringing stomach. He couldn't say yes or even O.K. He just numbly nodded his head.

The unrelenting voice tolled off the seconds: "1-2-3. Go!"

He peeled rubber. He snapped out the clutch,

99

stepped on the gas. The Model A leaped forward with a wild whine from its rear tires. Dave raced away from the stone bridge, shifted into second, not too smoothly, not too swiftly; tension and worry seemed to throw sand into the transmission; but he got into second, raced on up the hill. With his engine roaring he reached the first crest, double-clutched, shifted into high. His shifting was still a little noisy, jerky. Tromping the accelerator, he sent the Model A hurtling past Doc Brown's driveway up into the first loop of the S turn.

The night air rushed at him, banging bugs against the frail windscreen, slapping at his face. His eyes shut automatically just for a second, a defensive reflex against the onslaught of air. But why? His goggles should provide protection. Suddenly a fearful thought struck him; he had forgotten to pull his goggles down over his eyes!

The fearful thought stabbed into him like a hypodermic primed with irritating toxin. And the toxin spread swiftly through his body. He had been goaded into this challenge by Max Werner. He had let worry and irritation at the starting line spoil his preparation for the risky run. He had left his eyes unguarded and if he stopped to pull the goggles into position he would ruin his time for the hill climb.

Eyes blinking under a barrage of bugs, myriad specks magnified by his speed, he roared up into the

S turn, angry at himself, at Max, at the world. The red and white necklace of reflectors suddenly flung themselves at the Model A. Dave took his foot off the accelerator, hit the brakes, spun his wheels to the right.

The front wheels responded faithfully but the rear wheels kept rolling toward the reflectors.

The sound of the skid screamed up at him like a hysterical back-seat driver: You came into the turn too fast—you're going to crash!

Natural instinct prompted by fear told Dave to turn his wheels to the right, away from the menacing stone fence. But his driving skill fought through the fearful instinct and turned his front wheels into the skid. For the second time this maneuver stopped the front end of the Model A from fighting its losing battle with the rear end. But the whole car slid sideways, with its wheels clawing at the road like a mountaineer's fingers clinging desperately to a precipice.

Would he turn over? In a horrible moment Dave pictured his Model A demolished, junk once more. In that fearful time Dave thought not of himself but of the car he had constructed. And then, as if in answer to its owners' unselfish thinking, the Model A recovered its balance, got all of its wheels working again. And, although the momentum of the skid banged the tail of the hot rod against one of the boulders forming the fence, the car managed to respond to Dave's pressure on the accelerator. Scrambling back under control, it roared away from the stone fence and went rocketing off in the opposite direction.

Too much in the opposite direction. Now instead of rushing toward the stone fence and the ravine beyond it, Dave found himself plunging toward the sharp rock shelf that bordered the right side of the road. Never had that shelf of rock seemed so solid, so grim.

The headlights of the onrushing Model A heightened the frightening effect by illuminating the rock shelf's ugly crags and crevices, glistening evilly with wet stains and rivulets from seeping spring rains.

Heart pounding, eyes smarting, Dave braked hard, threw the wheel to the left. And once again he went into a skid as the head and tail of the Model A fought a battle for supremacy. Steer away from the rock! cried fear and instinct; but Dave ignored the panic-stricken cry and steered with the skid.

Would the maneuver work again? The only answer for the moment was the sobbing sound of the skid that raked Dave's nerves. He was out of control and he knew it. The pounding of his heart was no longer noticeable; that vital organ had apparently stopped in shock. His hands were frozen to the wheel, his eyes were blurred, his ears shrank from the impending crash. He cringed in the cockpit of the Model A like a terrorist who has lit the fuse of a bomb and is suddenly horrified by the monster he has set in motion.

He was in the skid for seconds; it seemed like hours. In each second—each hour—Dave tried to time a salvaging spurt out of the accelerator, a spin of the wheel, a sudden burst of speed that would pull the hot rod out of its fearful slide. But the sidewise skid was like a spinning gear whose whirring teeth refused to mesh. The right second for intervention by steering wheel and accelerator was agonizingly late in arriving. Too late. The Model A's rear wheels clawed courageously, obeying their master's desperate pressure on the accelerator. The front wheels obediently turned the way Dave wanted. But the hot rod's sidewise momentum was too great. With a horrible clang and crash the model A struck the rock shelf.

Collision. Its terrible noises assailed Dave's senses, ripped his pride. Fear faded before a wave of pity, a sense of shame, pity for the Model A, shame at his lack of skill. But the model A was still moving. With one last wrench, one last nauseating noise it came clear of the rock shelf like a wounded animal tearing itself out of a trap.

Dave braked to a stop, hands shaking, stomach churning. He was sick, mentally, physically—to think that he could drive the car he loved so recklessly that it would be ripped by a rock. And why? Because he had let himself be goaded into this crazy stunt by Max Werner. And for what? Worthless goals. The defiance of a constable and a hot rod record for an illegal hill climb. It didn't make sense.

Pulling on his emergency brake Dave reached for his flashlight. Trembling, he climbed out of the cockpit and fearfully sought out the damage. The shaky beam of light found a dent in the left rear fender—that was from the first collision with the stone fence on the other side of the curve. Not too bad. The flashlight's beam moved apprehensively toward the right of the car. Dave surveyed the damage—fenders wrinkled, ripped, crumpled. And the rear bumper bent back so far it was almost wrenched free. It was stupid, terrible, to abuse a car like that after working so hard to put it in shape.

The flashlight continued its examination and some of Dave's misery receded; for the wheels were undamaged, the tires intact. With a nimbleness gained from unlimited practice, Dave swung swiftly under the Model A, oblivious to his clothes or the car's risky slant. From axle to axle went the flashlight beam, slowly searching. His misery receded as he saw that everything was in place, firmly fastened.

Dave slid out from under, proud and reassured. His car was strong and sturdy—it could take it. The damage was really superficial—dented fenders, a bent bumper. Then why not go on with the hill climb, the challenge to Constable Currie? That would certainly impress the members of the Milltown Hot Rod Club.

How many of them would have the courage to race on after a smash-up?

As he hurried back behind the wheel Dave glanced up the hill. Lights were flashing—signals; Constable Currie had again set his speed trap at the cider mill. The Milltown hot rodders were on the job, cooperative but critical. And precious seconds were slipping away, Dave warned himself. So put on your goggles and peel rubber!

The Model A's tires screamed again as Dave tromped the accelerator. But he didn't maintain heavy pressure on the pedal—one damaging skid was enough. Driving carefully he negotiated the inside curve of the S turn with just a gentle whine from the tires. Dave felt better as he headed for the second outside corner. With his goggles on, the rushing night air no longer harassed his eyes. And his Model A had decisively demonstrated its sturdiness as well as its speed.

Just before negotiating the second outside corner Dave's eyes caught a flicker from his rear vision mirror. Headlights. Where the devil had they come from so suddenly? Cops? A slight twinge of apprehension plucked at nerves that had just stopped quivering. But the only cop in Branchville was Constable Currie. Those headlights probably belonged to some innocent driver of a pleasure car who had gained on the Model A when it skidded into the shelf of rock.

That pleasure car, some Stupid Six from Detroit with low-pressure tires and hydramatic transmission, would be left far behind, thought Dave proudly, as his hot rod roared up around the last curve of the S turn.

This last curve was taken at what Dave considered a speed far superior to that of the pleasure car. Roaring to the top of the hill, double-clutching, shifting smoothly into high, Dave grinned under his goggles; a pleasure car was no match for a hot rod. No sir. He would just glance in the rear-vision mirror to verify his own opinion. He looked, he gaped—headlights! They were still there, clinging, and clinging rather casually it seemed to Dave. They couldn't belong to a pleasure car—a Stupid Six from Detroit couldn't take that curve so fast. Then—who, what?—never mind. Outdistance it here on the flat straight road atop the ridge and at the same time humiliate Constable Currie. Open that cut-out—hit that gas pedal!

The wonderful noise returned, the brash roar of the engine in full cry, once more released from the restraint of its muffler. The swift rush of air whistled a thrilling song as the Model A raced toward top speed on the flat. Dave was swept away by that speed. There were no curves now to slow him down, send him skidding. This road on top of the ridge was made for wide-open speed and he roared over it wide open on a wild wave of intoxication. Forgotten now was the irritation over Max Werner, the smash-up on the rock-shelf curve, the suspicious headlights. Not only forgotten but outdistanced; a quick glance in the rear-vision mirror showed just two faint points of light. And as Dave watched, the two points disappeared entirely behind a pair of intervening headlights with a warning red light flashing—Constable Currie!

A shiver of apprehension skidded down Dave's back. The law! It never failed to stir up a thrilling flurry of fear. It added to all the excitement: the raucous noise of the unmuffled engine; the sounds and sensations of high speed. And now the chase; the road race against the constable; a perfect climax to the exciting hill climb.

Once more Dave grinned grimly under his goggles. Poor old Santa Claus—he was going to be humiliated a second time. Dave hoped the constable's car wouldn't break down again and spoil some of the fruits of victory. He glanced confidently in the rear vision mirror.

A flash of alarm shook his confidence. For the constable's car wasn't breaking down; its red light was flashing ominously nearer, nearer; it was gaining! Hunching over the wheel, Dave pushed the gas pedal down to the floor. His car responded gamely, raucously, violently. The brash roar rose wildly like the howling of a hurricane. It was the first time Dave's hot rod was wide open and he exulted in its fierce speed.

Not for long. His exultation was punctuated by the

107

flicker of a flashlight from the side of the road. What was that? The end of the measured mile—a signal from the hot rodder timing the run. How fast would the time be? If only he could have avoided that mishap on the S turn. Still his speed before and since was risky, record breaking.

Too risky? What was that slight wobble in the left front wheel? Where the devil had that come from all of a sudden? It wasn't good at any speed but at this terrific pace it was dangerous. But it would have to be tolerated till the town line was reached, for that red light was flashing relentlessly in the mirror. And now Dave could hear the eerie spine-chilling wail of the constable's siren sternly sobering the wild cry of the Model A's cutout.

The siren wailed menacingly in Dave's anxious ears, the red light flashed warningly in his rear-vision mirror. But his engine roared defiantly; the town line was now less than a mile away. And beyond that boundary was friendly territory in which Constable Currie had no jurisdiction.

Sweaty hands gripping the wheel, goggled eyes glued to the road, foot firm on the accelerator, Dave was throbbing through a wild world of exciting sensations, super speed, intoxicating sounds. Suddenly into this frenzied atmosphere shot a discordant noise that struck Dave's sensitive ears with the effect of a well-aimed bullet; the engine was missing; there was no more power in the gas pedal!

In a matter of seconds the Model A changed from a swift smooth thoroughbred into a bucking broncho. It kicked, missed, hissed. Steam rose, water sprayed against the windscreen.

Dave was shocked into sobriety. Shattered was the intoxicating world of exciting sensations. The wonderful engine was kicking, missing, steaming; the red light was flashing nearer and nearer, the siren wailing louder and louder.

Desperately pumping the gas pedal, Dave squeezed one last spurt from the engine. It carried the Model A to the top of the hill leading down to Chet Coley's filling station. He quickly threw in his clutch and disengaged the transmission, taking the gear drag off the Model A's forward speed and giving the hot rod a fast coast downhill.

For just a few seconds some of the speed sensations returned. But they were just shadows of their former selves. Now the rush of the night air was softer, slower, and the Model A was not backing belligerently off its pipes but sputtering indignantly.

Still Dave refused to give up. If he could just get one or two bursts of power out of the engine he could climb the hill ahead. And not far from the top of that hill was the town line—sanctuary.

With the clutch still in, sweaty hands gripping the

wheel, Dave stepped on the gas. *Ppphhhttt—ponk—ppphhhttt—ponk.* The engine sounded as if it were running under water. The red light flashed nearer, the siren wailed louder. Desperately Dave pumped the gas pedal, shifted into second, let out the clutch. *Arrur—ppphhhttt—ponk.* The Model A bucked past the filling station, staggered a few yards up the hill, gasped, and gave in. The end had come.

Constable Currie's car swung by with one last soul-shaking wail from its siren. A harsh voice yelled the classic phrase, "Pull over there!"

Crushed, completely defeated, Dave obeyed. There was nothing else to do. The Model A had expired; the race was finished; he had lost. He was going to be arrested. Arrested! No. His mind refused to accept the fact. This was all a horrible nightmare. He would wake up any minute now and hear his mother's voice from the other room, "Dave, what's the matter?"

But he didn't wake up. The red light on the constable's car continued to flash. The constable's horrible automobile had now stopped in front of the Model A, emphasizing the hot rod's defeat. Dave glared at the constable's car—how could a repulsive flatiron like that, a real Stupid Six, keep up with a streamlined hot rod? How? There suddenly seeped through Dave's anger and fear the suspicion planted by Max Werner—the constable's car had been souped up. It must have been. And who had done it—who had been the traitor?

Dave's angry question was answered by a third pair of headlights, the sound of a powerful engine purring, the gleam of a silvery exhaust coiling out of an awesomely long hood. The Stutz Bearcat had appeared from nowhere. From nowhere? Not exactly, Dave told himself, his anger rising. That blasted Bearcat was the car right behind me on the S turn. It was tailing me, cooperating with the constable.

Dave's anger overcame his anguish. He leaned out of the Model A and blew a Bronx cheer at the driver of the Bearcat.

Constable Currie hustled up triumphantly. "Young feller, are you gonna add insultin' an officer of the law to your long list of crimes and misdemeanors?"

Dave mumbled, "I wasn't talking to you. I was talking to that guy in the Stutz Bearcat."

"Humph," Santa Claus snorted. "If I was you, young feller, I'd keep my trap shut 'cause from here on everything you say can be used against you. And besides," Constable Currie fumbled eagerly for pencil and ticket, "it's not a Stutz Bearcat, it's a Duesenberg."

Duesenberg. That was it. For a moment Dave's love of engines and his knowledge of them obscured the horror and humiliation of the arrest. Of course it wasn't a Stutz Bearcat. It was a Duesenberg, the most wonderful car America had ever produced. One bet with

111

Max was won. One measly buck. How little it would matter beside the awful fines this arrest would cost, money that could have been spent to improve the Model A.

The horror and humiliation flooded back, swept over Dave, submerged him. He sank behind the wheel of his hot rod in a sickish self-pitying stupor. Automatically he handed over his license and registration. Numbly he heard Constable Currie say with satisfaction, "Speedin', reckless drivin', illegal use of cut-out. We're gonna throw the book at you, son. You hot rodders have been askin' for it and now by golly you're gonna get it!"

A feeble "So what?" struggled up from Dave's stupor. Let 'em throw the book at me. What did it matter? All was lost. Dave sank into a miserable silence again as the constable's voice continued to wash over him.

But suddenly Dave revived, for somebody was lifting the hood of the Model A. It was the traitor, the driver of the Duesenberg. How dared he touch the car he had betrayed? Dave's silent misery burst into an angry shout, "Take your blasted hands off my car!"

The shout had no effect. The hands, one holding a flashlight, continued to examine the stricken Model A.

Dave lunged from behind the wheel. "Listen you, I'm going t'—"

"You're going to stay right where you are." It was Constable Currie giving Dave a surprisingly strong push that dropped him back behind the wheel. And as he squawked angrily but ineffectually the deep voice of Webb Walden came over the windscreen, "You know what happened to your car, son? You blew the head gasket."

Blew the head gasket! So that was it. Of course. Mentally, mechanically, Dave could see the head gasket, a sheet of asbestos with holes for the cylinders. The head gasket fitted between the engine head and the block. When that gasket blew, water from the cooling system worked into hot cylinders where the gas was being burned, turned into steam, wet the spark plugs, crippled the engine.

For a few seconds Dave was distracted from his anger and misery by mechanical thoughts about the blown gasket. Then anger and misery returned as Dave told himself that Webb Walden had not only conspired with the constable to murder the Model A but had then appointed himself medical examiner and calmly performed an autopsy on the victim. It was unjust—worse—infuriating. And Dave showed his fury vocally.

This caused Constable Currie to chuckle as he wrote out the ticket. "Seems to me, young feller, that this hot rod ain't the only thing that's blown a gasket tonight. Now you just calm down, get out of that hot rod, and get in a real automobile. We're gonna take a nice slow ride to the police station."

It was a slow ride but it wasn't nice—far from it.

As Constable Currie drove back at a legal speed over the route which had been traversed so recklessly, the full weight of the disaster crushed down on Dave. He had been caught red-handed, captured. He wasn't being given a ticket for speeding and then sent home to appear in court on some future date. This was much more serious. "They" were going to throw the book at him. They might let him out on bail but perhaps bail would be set so high he wouldn't be able to raise it. Maybe his mother—at the thought of his mother Dave's misery multiplied; she would die a thousand deaths over this disgrace.

They were driving down Dead Man's Hill. Constable Currie sat straight and self-righteous behind his wheel, braking carefully, lowering his lights at the curves. Slumped in the seat, Dave numbly recognized the corner where he had collided with the shelf of rock. If only he had stopped right there and gone home on back roads. But no, he was afraid to be called "chicken" for not defying the law. In his misery, riding downhill in the police car, Dave faced the bitter truth—that he was chicken for another reason, for letting Max and the hot rodders goad him into the stupid stunt that had smashed up his Model A, blown a gasket, disgraced his mother, and placed him, Dave, in the custody of a vengeful policeman.

He had learned his lesson too late.

Chapter XI

WEBB WALDEN gently dropped the hood on the Model A and started toward his own car. He was smiling a little. For his inspection of the Model A's engine had not only shown the cause of its failure but revealed surprisingly good mechanical work. And with what a strange variety of parts! That curious water pump, that odd generator—they must have been resurrected from automobile graveyards. In fact, the whole contraption looked as if it had been brought back to life by a miracle of mechanical science. Many months of stubborn, persistent work must have gone into it. Ability plus work should equal what? Something worthwhile. But in this case it had all been

115

wasted on a wild ride, a crazy burst of defiance against law and order.

Webb Walden's smile had turned into a frown. It irked him to see promising mechanical talent squandered so thoughtlessly. But there was nothing Webb could do about it. The boy had defied the law and when caught he had blown up just like his car. A kid who behaved like that was a nuisance to the community, a menace to other drivers. And that wasn't all. Every time a fresh kid like that baits a constable, thought Webb, legitimate road racing is run into a ditch and some poor sucker like me has to sweat and struggle to get it righted again.

With these sober thoughts Webb Walden climbed into his Duesenberg, listened proudly to its powerful purr, turned around and drove back to the center of Branchville to see what Constable Currie had done with his prey.

But what had happened to the prey, now that he was in the Branchville police station? Why, he didn't look like the same young man at all. Gone was the loud, angry defiance. In its place was silent misery. What a sorry looking brat he was, with his thin lanky frame slumped on that crude bench, his back humped against the stained wall, the head that badly needed a haircut slumped on the leather jacket. Webb Walden noted the dirty fingernails, the grease-stained trousers and shoes, trademarks of the mechanic. And for the first time Webb felt a flash of pity. You poor dope, he thought, you asked for it and now you're going to get it.

Constable Currie was parading self-righteously in front of his prey, sputtering out law after law, penalty after penalty. And the prisoner sat slumped on the bench, silent and submissive, his thin face getting whiter as the verbal blows beat down that bushy head with the ridiculous sideburns: "Illegal use of the cut-out, speeding, reckless driving."

The prisoner was mumbling something without looking up.

Constable Currie lashed out at his victim. "You keep your big mouth shut! You've shot it off enough, under-stand? I'm doin' the talking from here on—get it?"

The prisoner mumbled, "— just wanted to go to the bathroom."

Constable Currie snorted. "Humph! Trying to pull a fast one, ay? Well son, lemme tell you, the bathroom window in here is no bigger'n a doughnut and it's barred and I'll be standing right outside the door with my gun ready. Understand, young feller?"

Webb Walden saw the bushy head nod. Webb noticed that the chalk white face now had a touch of green and that the mumble was more urgent. "Got t' go quick."

Constable Currie's beard bristled. "You'll go when I say you can go."

Webb Walden stepped up and spoke quietly in the constable's ear. "Better let him go now, Constable; I think he's going to be sick to his stomach."

"Ay?" For a moment Constable Currie looked as if he had never heard of anyone getting sick to his stomach. But when the implications sank in he acted quickly, almost frantically, "Go ahead son, go ahead. It's right over there in the corner."

The prisoner departed hurriedly and Constable Currie rubbed his whiskers and said, "Well, bless my soul. Look at that hard-boiled hot rodder, that juvenile delinquent. Humph. Guess I gave him a good scare, Webb."

"Guess you did, Constable," said Webb. "Well, I'll be running along. What do you plan to do with your prisoner, Constable, let him out on bail?"

"Mebbe," laughed Constable Currie. He tugged at his whiskers. "Wouldn't do him any harm to spend a night in jail."

Webb Walden said nothing.

"What I might do," continued Constable Currie, "is set the bail so high he won't be able to furnish it, say a fifty-dollar bond, somethin' like that. Got to teach these young squirts a lesson, Webb."

"Guess so," said Webb thoughtfully. And he said to himself, it's too bad. The kid has promising mechanical talent and he winds up in jail. Tough. But he certainly asked for it. Aloud Webb said, "Well, it's time to go home. Good night, Constable."

"Good night Webb," Constable Currie said. "By gum, you sure did me a favor when you souped up my car. Maybe I can help you out sometime."

"Maybe you can," said Webb smiling. "Good night."

Webb's wife, a redhead named Hortense, was sitting up in bed when her husband came home. But she was not asleep as Webb hoped she would be. She was wide awake and full of questions, "Who won the road race this time?"

"Constable Currie," said Webb, taking off his sweater.

"Well, good for him. Think he'll let you put on a hill climb now?"

"Maybe," said Webb, unbuttoning his shirt.

"What happened to the hot rod?"

"Broke down," said Webb, taking off his shirt.

"What kind of a car was it?"

"Model A," said Webb, retreating to the bathroom.

But the questions entered with him. "What was its driver like?"

"Tall skinnny kid—needs a haircut." Webb started brushing his teeth.

"That's a brilliant description of a human being," snapped Hortense. "What was his attitude like?"

"Sh-attitude?" said Webb through toothpaste and toothbrush.

"Yes, you big ox!" cried Hortense. "His attitude. Was he fresh, defiant? Did he look retarded—rejected? Did he act like a juvenile delinquent?"

Webb removed his toothbrush, parried the questions. "Have you by any chance been reading another book on child psychology?"

"Never mind what I've been reading," cried Hortense. "Tell me about the boy who got arrested."

The toothbrush went to work again. "Lishen, you know what teen-agers are like sheese days. You read sh-newshpapers." The brush stopped again to give its operator better diction for the crux of his argument, "You read that F.B.I. report in the papers." Webb's voice, normally deep, slow, and calm, raised its pitch, quickened its pace. "The increases in drinking and drug addiction are bad enough but what really burned me up was the big increase in traffic offenses among teen agers—up 45 per cent for 1952 over 1950." Webb stepped to the bathroom door, waved his toothbrush at his wife. "Up 45 per cent," he repeated. "How about that?"

"I didn't ask for an F.B.I. report," snapped his Hortense. "I asked—"

"But I'm giving you one!" cried Webb. "There's something wrong with the youth of this country and you know it. You read that report too, you saw the figures. Teen-agers are acting like irresponsible brats. I don't care if they break their own fool necks but when they endanger mine and yours and those of our kids then I get good and mad!"

"All right, all right," soothed Hortense, "so do I."

"Well then," said Webb, waving his toothbrush, "what are you going to do about it?"

"Stop waving that toothbrush at me," said his wife, "and tell me what *you* are going to do about it."

"Me?" cried Webb, "I've already done something. Didn't I help Constable Currie catch that teen-age traffic violator?"

"What's so wonderful about that?" cried Hortense. "He's caught, he's arrested, he's brought to trial, he's fined. In other words, he's punished. And what did punishment ever prove?"

"Plenty!" cried Webb. "Teen-agers like the kid caught tonight are like foul balls—they have to be straightened out."

"All right," cried Hortense, "but is arresting them, threatening them with jail going to cure the problem?"

"Who said anything about throwing them in jail?" said Webb defensively.

"I said threatening, not throwing," said his wife and then asked suspiciously, "Why?"

"Noshing." The toothbrush was moving again, slurring his words as Webb returned to the bathroom sink, mumbling to himself.

But not alone this time. Hortense leaped out of bed and was right behind him. "What are you mumbling about?"

"Noshing."

"For heaven's sake, take that toothbrush out of your mouth!"

Webb took the toothbrush out, turned, and, speaking in a flat tone, said, "Well, as a matter of fact, I feel sort of guilty."

"Why?" snapped his wife.

"Well, I was a kid once myself," Webb mumbled.

"What makes you think you still aren't?" snapped Hortense. "Listen, Webb, you don't feel guilty about helping a poor old constable bedeviled by juvenile delinquents. You feel guilty about something else. What?"

"Well, uh—" Webb wiped toothpaste off his mouth —"I'm not so sure this kid is a juvenile delinquent. I could see he'd done some darned good work on his Model A and he was so scared in the police station that he got sick."

"He got sick?" cried Hortense. "He certainly doesn't sound like a juvenile delinquent." Her voice sharpened. "Where is this terrible criminal now—out on bail, I suppose."

"Well, uh." Webb cleared his throat. "S'matter of fact, dear, I think he's in the clink. You see the constable thought a night in jail might—"

"Jail!" cried Webb's wife, advancing on her husband. "For a kid so scared he got sick? Are you out of your mind, Webb Walden?"

"Now listen, dear," said Webb, backing up against the sink, "I didn't—"

"You didn't what?" cried his wife, jabbing a finger against her husband's chest. "You didn't protest, Webb Walden. You just stood there like a dumb baboon while a scared, sick kid got railroaded to jail."

"Railroaded?" repeated her husband. "Now just a minute. He may not even be in jail. The bail was only fifty bucks."

"Fifty bucks!" cried Hortense. "And where in the name of heaven is a scared, sick kid going to get fifty bucks at this time of night?"

"Don't ask me," mumbled her husband.

"I'm not asking you," cried Hortense, jabbing Webb's chest with her finger, "I'm telling you. *You're* going to put up that bail."

"Me?" said Webb, jabbing himself with his finger.

"Yes, you!" cried his wife. "What have you got in that chest of yours—a heart or a carburetor?"

"Huh?" said her husband.

"You heard me!" cried Hortense. "You're going to post that fifty-dollar bond and then you and I are going to drive that boy home where he belongs and have a long talk with his parents."

"Gee, won't they be pleased," Webb mumbled.

123

"Never mind about that. You put on your shirt and sweater and get ready."

"How about you?" said Webb with a thin grin. "You going in your nightgown?"

"And don't try to be funny!" cried Hortense, snorting and stomping around the bedroom. "All this guff you've been handing out about teen-agers going to the dogs! And what have you done about it? Not one single solitary thing. Well, here's your chance, Webb Walden."

"How is it my chance?" said Webb, slowly putting his shirt back on.

"Because you're going to put up that bail!" cried Hortense. "You'll be investing in a juvenile delinquent who just happens to be a promising mechanic, who is so fierce a desperado that he gets scared sick at the police station. You'll want to make sure this criminal of yours shows up for his trial so you can get your bail back. So while you're waiting for his trial you can put him to work in your shop and see if you can beat some sense into his head."

"Now listen, dear," said Webb, buttoning his shirt.

"You listen to me, Webb Walden," cried his wife. And she talked on as Webb sighed and said to himself, seems to me that all I've been doing for the last few years.

Suddenly a thought occurred to him, a rescuing thought which he voiced hopefully. "Who's going to stay with the children, dear? Don't you think I'd better be the baby sitter?"

"Humph," snorted Hortense. "That's the first time you ever volunteered for that job. But I see through you and you're not going to baby-sit tonight. The baby sitter is going to be your assistant, Angus MacKenzie."

"But Angus is a mechanic, not a baby sitter," Webb protested.

"We've used him before," said Hortense, "and we'll use him again. You know Angus; when it comes to making a dollar he can never refuse even if it's earned at baby sitting."

Chapter XII

THE heavy door creaked on its hinges. Dave looked up and stared resentfully at Constable Currie. "Warden" Currie.

"Put up a fifty-dollar bond," the warden had said, "or you'll spend the night in jail."

The size of the sum had staggered Dave. Where would he get fifty dollars at this time of night? From Ma? No. It was the last thing he'd ask her to do. Then Dave had thought of the hot rod club—Max Werner. Warden Currie had permitted the phone call. But Max had said in a shocked voice, "Fifty bucks? Gee whiz, Dave, I couldn't put up more than five."

"Well, take up a collection among the members of the club."

"At this time of night?" whined Max. "Gee, it's awful late to be callin' fellas up askin' 'em for money."

"Listen," cried Dave angrily, "what kind of a president of the hot rod club are you anyway?"

"Now keep your shirt on, Dave," said Max soothingly.

"Aw, go bag your head," said Dave and hung up. He felt sick and weak again. And Constable Currie didn't help, standing near the phone pulling at his beard and saying, "Fine feathered friends you've got, Dave. Real friends in need those hot rodders, yes sir."

Dave winced.

"Better make some more calls," said Constable Currie. "You've got a family, haven't yuh?"

"I've got Ma," said Dave in a low voice, "but I'd rather spend a night in jail than ask her to put up a fifty-dollar bond." He pleaded, "Gee whiz, Constable, couldn't you give me a break just this once? I'll show up for the trial, I promise."

"Humph," Constable Currie snorted. "You teen-age twerps are all alike. You're fresh and sassy; you make noisy nuisances out of yourselves; you break one law after t'other; but when you get caught you just don't want to take your medicine."

All this had taken place an hour ago. The heavy door had swung shut on Dave's hopes. Now it was opening again and Warden Currie was standing there saying, "O.K. Dave, you can go."

"What?" Dave couldn't believe his ears.

"I said you can go," said Constable Currie coldly. "Somebody posted the bond."

"Who?" said Dave, getting slowly to his feet.

"You'll see," said Constable Currie.

He saw. It was the man who had souped up the constable's car, the traitor, Webb Walden. And his wife was with him, a redhead in sweater and slacks, with her hair in curlers.

Dave's mind battled with conflicting emotions— gratitude to Mr. Walden for posting the bond, resentment for the part Mr. Walden had played in the arrest. The battle was a stand-off and, as a result, Dave's attitude toward his rescuers was reserved. He thanked them for their intervention but his tone was cool. He accepted their offer of a ride to his crippled car but he sat by himself in the back seat brooding, a miserable mixture of remorse and resentment.

They drove up Dead Man's Hill and Dave tried to ignore the striking comparison—the way Webb Walden and the Duesenberg took the hill compared to Dave Neil and his Model A. Dave hated to admit it but Mr. Walden and the Duesenberg did a better job of shifting, turning, accelerating. They reached the top of the hill quickly and Mr. Walden, without turning his head said, "Ever ride in a Duesenberg before, Dave?"

"No sir," said Dave. (But I knew it was a Duesenberg. Max Werner was all wet as usual.)

Mr. Walden shifted smoothly and said, "Like it?"

"Yes sir." (Gosh, how smoothly he shifted. It's some car. I'll admit that any day. But what kind of a guy was the driver?)

"Ever hear of the Sports Car Club, Dave?"

"No sir." (What good were clubs anyway. You got in a jam on account of their initiation stunts and then they deserted you.)

"We put on hill climbs and road races too, Dave, but we do it legally. We get permission from the authorities first."

Dave said nothing except to himself. Legal hill climbs and road races. Gosh, that would be wonderful. But did Mr. Walden have to make a lecture out of it? We do it "legally"; "we get permission from the authorities first." Okay, rub it in. I was wrong; I admit it.

Now the voice from the front seat was feminine. "Have you any brothers and sisters, Dave?"

"No ma'am." (Snoopy dame, isn't she?)

"Father and mother living?"

"Just Ma." (Gosh, how snoopy can you get?)

He had time to say that he was seventeen and a high school junior before the Model A was reached and the investigation ended. The Model A stood crippled by the side of the road; Dave's heart went out to it; how sad it looked.

129

As the Duesenberg came to a stop Webb Walden said, "Let's get some water for your car, Dave, so you can drive it home."

Chet Coley's filling station furnished the water. While Dave poured it in, Mr. Walden examined the engine with his flashlight. Dave watched, half resentfully, half anxiously.

"Hmm," said Mr. Walden. "Interesting—lot of possibilities."

Dave stopped pouring water as a question tripped to the tip of his tongue. "What kind of possibilities, Mr. Walden?"

Mr. Walden chuckled maddeningly. "What kind? That will depend on you, Dave."

"Humph," Dave spilled water. (Wise guy, this Mr. Walden. Got you interested, then snubbed you.) Dave screwed the cap on the radiator and said, "Thanks for the lift, Mr. Walden. Guess I can get home all right from here."

Webb Walden smiled, "I'll follow you just to make sure."

Dave frowned. "You don't have to do that."

Suddenly Dave found himself blinking in the flashlight's beam as the voice behind it said coldly, calmly, "Listen Dave, I've got money invested in you—fifty dollars; and all I know about you is that you're a teenager who drives around breaking traffic laws. In other words, Dave, you're not a very good risk. And to make

130

you a better risk I'm going to go home with you and have a talk with your mother."

Dave sputtered. So did his Model A. It limped along like an ailing Pekinese followed by a healthy bulldog. Dave was sore, disillusioned; the sickness in his stomach had spread to his heart. Everything had gone wrong—all his wonderful dreams had been shattered. When he reached home all he could say to his startled mother was, "Some people want to see you, Ma." Then he ran upstairs, locked the door to his room, quickly got into bed, and, like an ostrich hiding its head in sand, pulled the covers over his head.

Now the voices rising from the living room were doubly muffled and he could hardly distinguish his mother's from Mrs. Walden's. What the heck were they yakking about down there? The question was completely rhetorical for it was plain that they were talking about the past, present, and future of one Dave Neil. The nerve of those Waldens butting in like this, thought Dave. Oh sure, it was nice of them to post the fifty-dollar bond, but gee whiz, that didn't give them the right to move in and take over. Lot of nerve. Dave snorted into the pillow. But Ma could handle them. She'd tell them where to get off.

Slowly, in the security of his own home, in the warmth of his own bed, Dave's self-confidence returned.

131

Webb Walden and his wife were driving home in the Duesenberg. Webb was silent for a while but as they crossed the town line he said in his slow voice, "Well, I told you so."

"Told me what?" said his wife.

"He's a mother's boy," said Webb calmly.

"Humph," Hortense snorted. "Anything to blame it on a woman. Is it that poor widow's fault that her husband died six years ago?"

"Of course not," said Webb as they passed Chet Coley's filling station. "But you know as well as I do that too many mothers spoil their sons. There's even a name for it—momism."

"Nonsense!" cried his wife. "For every mother who spoiled her son there's a father who spoiled his daughter. And what about all those mothers who made men out of their sons and kept the home fires burning while paw was off doing something noble like catching trout or shooting ducks?"

Webb sighed into silence. What was the use of arguing with Hortense—you could never win. It was better to talk on uncontroversial subjects like, er, how a high-compression head would help Dave's Model A. As he explained what a high-compression head would do, Hortense shook her head.

"Sometimes I wonder," she said.

"About what?"

132

"I wonder why men like you and boys like Dave Neil get such a big kick out of auto engines."

"Well," said Webb slowly, "I think it's because the auto engine satisfies two strong male instincts: one, curiosity—what makes that engine run; two, a desire to improve something, to make that engine perform better."

"I see," said Hortense. "And you share these instincts with Dave Neil?"

"I suppose so," said Webb.

"Well, then," cried his wife, "that's all the more reason why you should help Dave out of the jam he's in."

"Now wait a minute," said Webb, steering the car over the stone bridge, "I posted that fifty-dollar bond didn't I? And incidentally, why didn't Mrs. Neil put up that bond?"

"Dave was probably too proud to ask her," said Hortense.

"Maybe," said Webb, "but I thought there was a law making the parents of the delinquent post the bond."

"In some communities there is," said Hortense, "but not in this one. Branchville has a very primitive judicial system."

"Whew." Webb whistled as he guided his sports car past the town hall. "I hope our prosecuting attorney, Amos Sefton, didn't hear you say that."

"I wouldn't care if he did," said Hortense sharply. "Amos Sefton means nothing to me. He's just a dairy farmer who charges too much for his milk."

"Amos Sefton," said Webb, his voice rising and quickening, "is a smart cookie who will be the key man in this case."

"If he's so smart why is he a dairy farmer?" sniped Hortense.

"Because he prefers it to practicing law," said Webb hotly. "Listen, just because a guy doesn't spout all that stuff about kids being 'rejected' and 'retarded' and 'insecure' doesn't mean he won't use a lot of common sense when he comes to a case involving some teen-aged brat. Amos is shrewd enough to tell the difference between a kid who has criminal instincts and one who just got out of line temporarily."

"We'll see," said Hortense. "If your Amos is such a Socrates then we have nothing to worry about. But personally I'd put a lot more faith in the trial justice, Roger Thaxter. Of course he's in New York most of the time but I know his wife Helen in the P.T.A. and I might—"

"Don't try to tip the scales of justice," warned Webb, "they might tip the wrong way."

"Nonsense," snapped Hortense. "I could prepare a report on the case and have Helen give it to Roger."

"Listen," said Webb firmly, "you got me into this thing—it's my fifty bucks that's been posted, it's my workshop that's going to guide the defendant Dave Neil. So let me handle it in my own strange way."

"All right," said Hortense, "but just see that you handle it."

"Don't worry," said Webb. "I'll handle it. And if there are going to be any reports on the case they'll be given first to Constable Currie and then to Amos Sefton. I'm not going to go over their heads and make them my enemies before or during the trial."

Chapter XIII

DAVE heard the front door close. The voices faded and a wonderful sound rose to Dave's bedroom window—the growl of the Duesenberg. Gosh that was a powerful car. Too bad it belonged to—oh well, he was gone and good riddance. He would have to be seen again just once more at the trial. Then good-by for good.

"Dave."

It was his mother's voice just outside the bedroom door. Dave didn't like the sound of it. It had a disturbing, new quality, a determined firmness.

"Are you asleep, Dave? I don't think you are. I don't see how you could be, after the trouble you've caused tonight."

Dave scowled and burrowed his head under the pillow. O.K., he said to himself, I'm not asleep. So what? But I'm going to pretend to be. I'll be gosh-darned if I'm going to listen to any more lectures.

But the pillow, even arranged like ear muffs, could not keep out the sound of his mother's voice. That irritating new tone penetrated like an X-ray. It talked about being ashamed, about being shocked. That was to be expected. But what was it saying now? The scowl left Dave's mouth; it opened in astonishment while the pillow came off one stricken ear. "Starting tomorrow after school, Dave, you're going to work for Mr. Walden as an apprentice mechanic."

"*What!*" Dave squawked a protest as he jackknifed to a sitting position in his bed. "Work for that rich snoopy snob!"

"I thought you were just pretending to be asleep," said his mother firmly. "Now you just listen to what I have to say."

Listen, listen. They all wanted him to listen, the constable, Mr. Walden, and now Ma. Dave was scowling again. But he didn't hide his head under the pillow. He listened.

"You ought to be thanking your lucky stars, Dave, that you've found such a fine new friend as Mr. Walden."

Fine new friend my eye, said Dave to himself. Who souped up the constable's car?

"To think," said the new tone, "that Mr. Walden, a complete stranger, would post a fifty-dollar bond to keep you from going to jail."

Sure, said Dave to himself, he posted it all right. And he's so scared he's going to lose it he's following me like a hawk after a chicken. He not only followed me home and handed Ma a lot of propaganda but now he's got me signed up as an apprentice mechanic. *Me*, an apprentice! Look at the work I did on my Model A, the best little hot rod in Milltown. 'Course it did blow a gasket but—

"Things are going to be different from now on, Dave," said the new tone. "This terrible business has shown me that I've been too lenient with you."

"I suppose Mr. Walden told you that, too," Dave mumbled.

"It's very plain to me now," said his mother sharply, "that you need some strong male guidance, Dave, man-to-man talks that I haven't been able to give you."

"Man-to-man talks my eye," Dave muttered. "Sermons, that's what they are. And from a snoopy rich snob."

Dave repeated that phrase over and over again. It was like counting sheep. He tried to put his conscience to sleep with it after his mother's voice had gone from the door. "Snoopy rich snob." But the conscience refused to be lulled. Was Webb Walden really such a bad guy? He had posted that bond. And whose fault

138

was it that laws had been broken? Who had used the cut-out, exceeded the speed limit, driven recklessly? Not Webb Walden in his Duesenberg. The devil had to be given his due; Mr. Walden was a good driver and that was a wonderful car he owned. Humph. Dave snorted again. But who did all the dirty work on it? Webb Walden? Naw. Some guy like me, Dave told himself. Sure. And that's what I'll be doing from now on—the dirty work.

When he reported for work the next afternoon Dave expected to see a sign "Service Entrance" marking a driveway under stately trees; a maid in uniform coming to the kitchen door answering his query in a haughty voice, "The garage? It lies just beyond the tennis court before you get to the swimming pool."

But there was no sign saying "Service Entrance," just a mail box with the name Walden. The house was neat but small. The driveway was of plain dirt. It curved up through a grove of white birch trees and disappeared over a hill behind the house. There was no sign or sound of mechanical activity.

Dave stood and stared at the unexpected scene. The whole place was a great disappointment. It destroyed his image of Webb Walden as a rich snob; at least he wasn't rich. And its obvious lack of mechanical equipment—why it couldn't even be classed with a filling station—left Dave feeling flat and disinterested.

A call from the house startled him. It was Mrs. Walden. She was still in a sweater and blue jeans—hadn't she even gone to bed? Well at least the curlers were out of her red hair so she didn't look so silly; in fact, she wasn't bad looking, Dave had to admit. But, by gosh, she sure had acted like a busybody. And if there was anything worse than a disloyal friend like Max Werner then it was a female reformer like Mrs. Walden. So Dave was reserved and suspicious as he approached the house.

But he found nothing of the reformer in Mrs. Walden's manner. She didn't say, "Now Dave you've been a bad boy but we *understand* you and we're going to try to help you. And *you* must try and help *too*." There was none of that malarkey. All she said was, "Hi Dave, you're probably hungry. How about a piece of pie before you go to work?"

Dave's mouth dropped open and when it closed it bit into the juiciest deep-dish apple pie he had ever tasted. A glass of cold milk went with it. And some rather interesting conversation:

"You won't be working with Webb today, Dave. He's in New York. While Webb is away," said Mrs. Walden, "you'll be working for his assistant, Angus MacKenzie."

"Angus MacKenzie?" Dave repeated the name. "What's he like, Mrs. Walden?"

Mrs. Walden smiled and put a little burr in her

140

voice. "Angus is a dourrr Scot but his barrrk is much worrrse than his bite." She laughed lightly. "Some people think Angus is a grouch but he's, well, just slightly eccentric. You'll get along all right with Angus if you just keep your mouth shut and do what you're told."

"Yes ma'am," said Dave, swallowing.

"Angus is not what I would call a congenial soul," said Mrs. Walden, "but he does warm up on one subject."

"Auto engines?" asked Dave.

"No," smiled Mrs. Walden, "baseball."

"Oh," said Dave, and added hopefully, "the Yankees and Mickey Mantle?"

Mrs. Walden frowned. "No, I believe it's the Dodgers and Jackie Robinson."

Dave groaned.

Mrs. Walden ignored the groan. "Well," she said, "you'd better be on your way. Angus will be waiting for you."

"Yes ma'am," said Dave. He wiped his mouth on a paper napkin and started for the kitchen door. "Thank you very much for the pie, Mrs. Walden."

"Don't mention it. Oh, one more thing, Dave." Her words caught up with him as he departed. "I don't know what kind of a mechanic you are but Angus and Webb will treat you as an apprentice. In other words for the first few days you'll be doing the dirty work,

141

fixing flats, flushing radiators, charging batteries. And if I were you, Dave, I wouldn't complain about it."

Dave swallowed again, "Yes ma'am. Thanks for the advice."

She was smiling again. "You'll find the workshop over that hill." She pointed in the direction of the birch trees. "Good luck."

"Thanks for everything," he said and walked away.

Conflicting thoughts accompanied him. Mrs. Walden wasn't so bad. She didn't seem to be a reformer and she made wonderful pie. And it was darned nice of her to give that warning about Angus MacKenzie. A dour Scot, slightly eccentric; and a Dodger fan of course—didn't the two go together?

Dave walked quickly up through the grove of birches, reached the top of the hill, stopped, and stared down at Webb Walden's workshop.

It lay in a pocket of land, a small shallow valley. It looked like a crude assembly line. On the left in an open lot crouched a motley collection of rusty cast-offs, crumpled hulks, dingy derelicts. In the center stood a big cinder-block garage. And on the right waited an open shed with a tin roof and cars covered with canvas. Did the junk on the left go through the garage and come out in the shed ready to roll? If it did, Dave told himself, then Webb Walden and Angus MacKenzie were not only accomplished but determined mechanics—brothers under the skin. Hopeful, even enthusiastic, Dave hurried down the hill and entered the garage.

"Where the divil have you been?" It was a growl almost as gravelly as Honest Harold's, and it came up from the garage floor. In fact, Dave almost stepped on it.

A torso had come sliding out from under a car on a dolly, a flat wooden sled with four casters and a leather head rest. The upturned face on the dolly had a scrubby beard; a belligerent chin; sharp, deep-set eyes. The torso on the dolly was stocky and muscular and the dark blue coverall that enveloped it had the name Angus sewn in red script above a breast pocket.

Dave stared down at the strange sight. The face on the dolly scowled and Dave suddenly realized he hadn't answered its question. "In the h-house," he stuttered.

"And what the divil werre you doin' in the house?" growled the voice from the dolly.

"Eating p-pie," said Dave honestly.

"*What!*" The torso sat bolt upright. The voice roared. "What' d'you think we're rrunning here—a tea rroom!"

"No sir," said Dave timidly.

"Then you do your pie-eating at home, me lad," growled the voice from the dolly. "Now go get a coverall from that closet." The belligerent jaw jerked in the direction of a door in the rear. Then the voice growled on. "When you come from the closet turrn to yourr left and you'll find two flats. Fix them."

"Yes sir," said Dave heading for the closet. And to himself he said, this must be something like the army; maybe that old grouch on the dolly is an ex-sergeant. But I guess I'd better take Mrs. Walden's advice—do what I'm told and keep my mouth shut.

The coverall was well worn but clean and neatly patched in two places. But the flat tires looked dull and dirty. The dirty work, said Dave to himself, just as I thought. Why don't they give me something worth my salt like a ring job or replacing a head gasket? Gosh, when will I ever get my Model A fixed—not only the head gasket but that wobble in the front wheel? Dave groaned. And here I am stuck fixing flats while some cluck like Max Werner works on his V-8. It isn't fair.

What could be duller than fixing a flat? This one for instance. With a grunt Dave got the tire off the rim, turned it slowly in his hands. Where the heck was the puncture? No sign of it. Then inflate the tube, magnify the puncture, detect it by sight or sound. Where was the air hose? Ask Angus, the crabby Scot? No, better find it yourself.

Dave found the air hose, inflated the tube, listened, looked. No sound or sight of the leak. He scrounged some more, found a bucket, filled it with water, turned the tube in it slowly, one small section at a time. Suddenly, as the tube turned, bubbles floated up to the surface. The leak was a hole not much bigger than the head of a pin.

With his thumb marking the puncture, Dave took the tube with him and searched the workbench. He soon found the blow-out patch and the rubber cement to hold it. Then he gently roughed up the tube around the puncture with a piece of sandpaper and coated it with rubber cement. It was now ready for the patch to be pressed firmly in place. Then he went on to the second flat tire.

This time the puncture was easier to find. It was a short gash on the inside of the tube. Dave examined it closely. It wasn't the ordinary kind of puncture caused by a nail or jagged glass. Then what was it? Picking up the wheel from which he had pried the tire Dave ran his fingers over the rim. The fingers stopped on a rough spot, small but big enough under speed and pressure to cause a rim cut. That was it.

He had carefully smoothed out the rough spot by some strenuous scrubbing with a wire brush when a voice growled at him, "What's the trrouble, lad, rrim cut?"

Dave swung and towered over Angus MacKenzie: in a vertical position Angus was several inches shorter than Dave but it gave no feeling of superiority to the apprentice.

"Yes sir," said Dave, "rim cut. I've smoothed out the

145

rough spot but perhaps a rubber liner on the rim would—"

"Rright," growled Angus, "there's a drawer full of flaps at the end of the bench. Use one. When you finish that, grab those two batteries on the end of the bench, take 'em into the battery rroom"—the bearded, belligerent chin jerked in the direction of an annex— "check 'em and charrge 'em. Then rreport back to me."

"Yes sir," said Dave. He ran his finger over the rim and asked himself, Would this be a tactful time to bring up baseball—perhaps a casual mention of Jackie Robinson and the Dodgers? No, not now, later perhaps.

"Flaps," he found out, were rubber linings. He stretched one around the guilty rim. Then he patched the tube and went on to the batteries, thanking his lucky stars for the experience he had picked up with summer jobs in filling stations. Gosh, imagine saying to Angus, "I'm sorry, sir, but I don't know how to do it." Why the old Scot sourpuss would probably slug you with a wrench.

Fortunately the battery charger was a fairly familiar machine with its three red plastic dials and the needle of the meter that could point to either one of three panels: Defective, Recharge, Good.

The batteries Angus had indicated were old, their cell caps clogged with the ugly green and white discharge of battery acid. They didn't look as if they could take a charge but Dave knew that in the mechanical world looks were often deceiving. After carefully cleaning the terminals and checking the cells, he hooked on the leads. They had rubber caps with metal clamps inside. The red cup was positive, the black negative. Working the red plastic dials on the panel, Dave turned the selector to "test." For five minutes he gave the first battery a fast charge. Then he set the time to slow charge and turned the selector to "test." When five seconds had elapsed, he watched the needle on the panel. It moved to the left, pointing to the space marked "defective." No use charging that battery.

But the same test with the second battery moved the needle on the panel to "good." This one was worth recharging. So he set the timer to thirty minutes and rotated the rate selector to 100 amperes. This gave the second battery a fast charge.

Suddenly Dave heard the growl again. He turned apprehensively. But the dour face wore a warmer look. Evidently Angus MacKenzie was pleased with the way the apprentice was doing his work on the tires and batteries. The growl was softer as it burred, "While the batterry's charrging I want you to floosh out a rradiator."

"Yes sir." And to himself Dave said, Flush out a radiator. That does it. Just what Mrs. Walden warned me. Fix flats, flush radiators, charge batteries. Might as well be working in a filling station.

He was disgruntled. But at the same time he was proud of the work he had done so far and the beneficent effect it had had on Angus MacKenzie. The Scot was certainly not yet friendly but he looked much less irascible as he led the way out the rear door to the car to be worked on.

It was quite a car. Low, long, streamlined. Like the Duesenberg phaeton it had a "quad job," four carburetors. But this car had none of the comforts of the phaeton. It was just a two-seater and had obviously been built for one purpose—racing.

Fascinated Dave asked, "What kind of car is it, Mr. MacKenzie?"

"That, lad," said Angus, "is a hybrrid. We marrried a Forrd to a Duesenberrg."

"Ford—Duesenberg," said Dave impressed.

"Prrecisely. Ourr next special is going to be all Duesenberrg, that is if Mr. Walden has any luck tracking down that Model J today."

"Model J?" said Dave.

"Model J Duesenberrg," said Angus, "and marrk me words, lad, it was the finest engine iverr made in Indianapolis or iny other place fer that matterr." Angus was mellowing fast; there was butter on his burr now. "Why there werre only about five hundred Duesenberrgs made, lad. And they cost as much as thirty-seven thousand dollars apiece."

"Thirty-seven thousand dollars?" cried Dave in an awed voice.

"Rright, me lad. And take me word as a Scot who knows his values—the Duesenberrgs werre worrth everry dollar. Now if Mr. Walden locates a Model J today we'll be in luck, lad. We can make an all-Duesenberrg racing carr from it, enter it in Sporrts Car Club hill climbs and rroad rraces, have a lot of fun and at the same time brring in the business."

Dave nodded. He was beginning to see the light at last. This sports car business was complicated to say the least. He touched the Ford-Duesenberg respectfully and said, "And in the meantime this hybrid advertises your business?"

"That is it exactly, lad," said Angus. "We're getting the Ford-Duesenberrg rready for a hill climb in Verrmont—an exacting contest on a hairr-rraising rroad up Mt. Equinox."

"Up a mountain?" said Dave, awed again.

"Oh yes, lad," said Angus. "You'd have to see it to believe it. It's a terrible strrain on an engine's cooling system. All kinds of cars bubble up and boil over on Equinox. That's why you'll be working on this rradiator, lad. I want it reverrse-flooshed not just once but five times."

"Reverse-flushed?" Dave tripped on the phrase. First it was flush—now it was reverse-flush. To flush a radiator was simple enough. You opened the petcock at the bottom and flushed from the top with a hose—water pressure. But you couldn't reverse-flush with water from a hose; there wouldn't be enough pressure. Then how was it done? Air pressure? Probably. But better ask Angus. Filling station experience had taught Dave that unless you were absolutely sure it was better to admit ignorance or uncertainty and ask. Angus, the Scottish sourpuss, seemed to have sweetened; his answer to a humble question might be polite as well as helpful.

So Dave said, "I've never reverse-flushed a radiator, Mr. MacKenzie. Do you start at the bottom and use air pressure?"

"That's rright, Dave."

"Dave." Gosh, Angus was almost friendly. Mrs. Walden had been right. If you did your job well and kept your mouth shut, Angus was a reasonable man. In fact, he was now patiently explaining how a radiator was reverse flushed. First, you disconnected the hoses top and bottom and drained the radiator. Then you attached a separate hose at the top to carry the dirty water away from the engine. "Then," said Angus, "you take this reverrrse floosh attachment." And as Angus produced the attachment, Dave watched closely —flushing a radiator wasn't so dull after all.

The "reverse-flusher" was a comparatively simple but ingenious device which worked on one hundred pounds of air pressure. With this pressure behind it

150

the reverse-flusher could send a cleansing stream of air or water shooting up through the radiator, sending sediment and rust spurting out the hose attached to the top.

Psssst. Angus pulled the trigger and demonstrated the power of one hundred pounds of air pressure. Then he said, "Remember now, I want you to reverrse floosh it five times, lad, so we'll have a nice clean rradiator for that hill climb in Verrmont. If the Forrd-Duesenberrg overrheats at Equinox the blame will fall on your shoulders, lad."

"Yes sir," said Dave as Angus once more demonstrated the power of the reverse-flusher—*psssst.* As he watched, Dave got the idea that Angus was enjoying the lecture. The grouchiness was gone and the once-dour face seemed on the verge of a smile as if at long last the sun were about to rise and warm a bleak, dark land. Mrs. Walden, thought Dave, had been dead right; Angus' bark was much worse than his bite. And now perhaps, in this mellow moment, the topic of baseball might be profitably introduced. Now let's see, what team did Mrs. Walden say Angus liked? Oh yes, the Bums. And a particular player? Jackie Robinson.

Disconnecting the hoses on the Ford-Duesenberg, Dave smiled and said, "Well Mr. MacKenzie, it's almost time for the baseball season to open."

"That's rright," said Angus MacKenzie and the growl that once suggested pebbles pouring down a chute now sounded like a brook babbling happily over well-worn boulders.

Pleased with the reaction his tact had produced, Dave blithely tried some more of it. "Looks like the Dodgers have a good chance to cop the pennant again this year. That guy Jackie Robinson can really belt the—"

Pssssst. Dave staggered as if shot. In fact, he had been shot, in a way, by air pressure accompanied by a light but startling spray of water. And Angus Mac-Kenzie was scowling and growling again.

But why? Dave asked himself as he warded off another blast from the air hose. What have I done wrong? Were these Dodger fans completely crazy?

Dodger fans? Angus MacKenzie was growling at a great rate, "Listen, me lad, never mention the Dodgers around here agin—underrstind? They're not fit to reprresent the National League. Why, look how many times they got licked by the Giants last yearr. And will ye ever forget what the Staten Island Scot, Bobby Thompson, did t' them in the 1951 playoff? Will ye everr ferrget his mirraculous home rrun in the ninth— oh what a mighty blow that was! With one fell strroke it shatterred all the hopes of those terrrible imposterrs from Brrooklyn."

Imposters from Brooklyn. Bobby Thomson and his home run? Dave gasped as the full realization of his mistake struck home: because of a woman's ignorance of baseball he had insulted the most fanatical of all fans, a follower of the New York Giants. Holy crow!

Still raving about Bobby Thompson, Angus MacKenzie stomped off into the garage, leaving Dave alone to reverse flush the radiator of the Ford-Duesenberg. With a sigh Dave picked up the mechanism which had been fired like a pistol and, turning the valve, sent a stream of clean water shooting up through the radiator. It worked well. Rusty water sprayed from the hose at the other end, the pungent smell of anti-freeze floated through the soft spring air. Dave sighed again. He had wanted to get off on the right foot with Angus MacKenzie in the Walden workshop. He had kept his mouth shut, done the dirty work quickly, efficiently. And then bang, or rather, *pssst*. A slight conversational slip based on misinformation—and an improving relationship was back where it started from.

Dave turned off the water, switched on the air. *Pssst*. A gurgling stream turned into a geyser of rust-colored water. Dave watched, fascinated, as the reverse-flusher blasted all the grime and grit from the radiator. It was wonderful the way this thing worked. It wasn't such an uninteresting job and it was contributing to a very interesting cause—the preparation of the Ford-Duesenberg for that hill climb in Vermont. Gosh, wouldn't it be wonderful, thought Dave, if some day I could drive a car like this in an official hill climb like that—a "quad job" powering up a mountainside—

153

Wow! How could a man like Angus MacKenzie, working on cars like Ford-Duesenbergs, priming them for thrilling hill climbs, let himself get all steamed up about a team like either the New York Giants or the Brooklyn Dodgers. What the heck did it matter about those two teams anyway, thought Dave as he reverse-flushed the Ford-Duesenberg; whichever National League team won the pennant would be clobbered in the World Series by the Yankees and Mickey Mantle.

All things considered, Dave was somewhat surprised to be offered a ride home by Angus when the day's work was done. Angus apparently was a Scottish screwball whose moods were unpredictable, switching from grouchy to congenial like fitful weather changing from fair to foul. Now, at the end of the day, Angus seemed in a good humor. In fact, the car he chose for transportation was the Ford-Duesenberg which gave Dave the opportunity to ask questions about the hybrid's unusual features—that instrument on the dashboard for example.

"That's a tachometer, lad. For real high-speed driving you measure the revolutions perr minute instead of the miles perr hourr. It's a bit like baseball. The real experrts don't just look at the box score to see who wins—they watch the batting averages to see how the team is hitting. And if ye've got hitterrs like Bobby Thompson batting consistently over .300, why then

154

you know yourr team is deliverring its rpm's. Underr-stand?"

Dave understood all right. Now he knew why the Scot was suddenly so solicitous; he was a baseball missionary trying to convert "strays" to the cause of the New York Giants. Dave didn't mind that propaganda so long as it was preceded by information about the Ford-Duesenberg. So he kept asking questions and as he listened to the answers he separated the wheat from the chaff, the mechanical from the athletic.

"Special steering wheel? Rright. It has a rracing rratio—two turrns lock to lock. Compare that to a stock car's six. Your rracing rratio gives you quick rre-action with light touch so you don't have to go winding the wheel this way and that as if you were on a rruddy ship. It's like having a good catcher on a ball team who steers the ball club, keeps everrything tight arround the infield, holds the rrunners close to first and third. Like that catcher with the Giants, Wes Westrrum."

Smiling to himself Dave asked the correct position of the hands on the wheel. At the top?

"Ach, lad, not at the top," said Angus. "That would be all right for a wheel with six turns lock to lock. But compare your wheel to a clock, lad, and put your hands at nine o'clock and three o'clock. Of course the position is imporrtant like the position of your hands on a base-ball bat. Good ball players like the Giants automati-

155

cally put their hands in the right place whitherr they're hitting or fielding."

Dave ignored the part about the position of the hands on the bat and filed the information about the hands on the wheel—at nine o'clock and three o'clock. Then he continued to listen, fascinated by the engineering information, amused by the baseball propaganda, as Angus cleverly carried the analogy from one part of the Ford-Duesenberg to the next: domed pistons, oversize valves, racing camshafts. Impressed by the mechanical knowledge, Dave became so interested that he was surprised to look out suddenly and recognize his own home.

"Here we are," he said.

"Ach," said Angus braking, "so this is where you live. Aye, a nice little cottage."

The Ford-Duesenberg came to a stop and, as Dave got out after thanking Angus for the ride, he couldn't resist smiling and saying, "I'm sorry I mistook you for a Dodger fan, Mr. MacKenzie."

"Ah, that's all right, lad," said Angus indulgently. "We all make mistakes. If we didn't we wouldn't be human now, would we?" Angus shifted into first, revved up the Ford-Duesenberg's engine *arroom, arrroom*. It seemed to burr a little like the Scot at its wheel.

"It was Mrs. Walden who gave me the bum steer, Mr. MacKenzie. She didn't mean to but you know how some women are about sports—they get everything backward."

"Ah, women," said Angus with a philosophical sigh. "What would the worrld be without them?"

"Matter of fact, Mr. MacKenzie, you got me tagged wrong too. I'm not a Dodger fan—never have been."

"You're not!" Angus jerked up behind the Ford-Duesenberg's wheel. "Then by the tartan of Mac-Kenzie you must be a—"

Dave tried not to smile. "No, sir, I'm not a Giant fan. As a matter of fact I root for the Yankees and Mickey Mantle."

"*What!*" Angus MacKenzie was so shocked that he let out the clutch without pressing on the accelerator. The Ford-Duesenberg became just another car. It bucked, stalled. Cursing, Angus MacKenzie pressed the starter button, gunned the engine, *arrroom arroom.* The Ford-Duesenberg responded with a full-throated roar that rocked Dave Neil back on his heels. And then as the noise of the engine moderated, the voice of Angus MacKenzie growled, "A Yankee fan, ay? So you just cheer for the winners, the rich man's club. You know how they win their pennants—with their bankroll—the almighty dollar. The plutocrrats of baseball!" Angus was sputtering like a wet spark plug. "Oh, they couldn't have an ordinary ball park like the Polo Grounds or even Ebbets Field. Oh no, the plutocrrats have to have a ruddy stadium. Well,

157

me lad, you know what's happened to the dollar—it's lost 50 per cent of its value. And that's what will happen to a team that's bought and built with dollars. And as for that upstart Mickey Mantle—"

Arrooomm. Unable to think of an appropriate insult, Angus covered his angry lapse with a blast from the Ford-Duesenberg and roared away into the night.

Chapter XIV

EYES wide, mouth open, Dave watched the Ford-Duesenberg roar away toward Branchville. What a powerhouse that was and what a strange character drove it—a real screwball was Angus MacKenzie; undoubtedly a fine mechanic and a good man at heart but a real nut, the most fanatical fan of all, a follower of the New York Giants. Dave shook his head, sighed, and smiled. Imagine being mistaken for a Giant fan. Gosh, that was funny, it really was. Dave laughed. And then stopped laughing as a voice said, "Hi Dave."

He swung around, peered through the darkness. It wasn't Angus MacKenzie. This voice had no burr. It had a bossy swagger to it, something that gave Dave an uneasy feeling in the pit of his stomach. He automatically clenched his fists as he stared at the shadowy figure that had stepped around the far corner of the house. It was Max Werner.

Speaking to Max on the telephone from the police station, Dave could be contemptuous. But a face-to-face meeting was different. All Dave managed to say was "Hi."

"Wanted to see you for a minute, Dave." The voice was tough, cocky, as its owner swaggered from the shadows, showing the jaunty cap, the leather jacket, the elaborate glass work on the motorcycle belt glittering in a ray of light from Dave's home.

Dave swallowed. "What about?"

"Certain guy came to see me."

"That so?"

"Yeah, that's so. Know who he was?"

"Haven't any idea."

"That rich snob Webb Walden."

Dave said nothing.

"How'd he get my name, Dave?" The voice threatened.

"I dunno Max, honest I don't."

"You're sure?"

"Absolutely."

"Humph. You'd better be." Max hooked his thumbs in his belt. "Walden tried to scare me. But I don't scare easy, understand? You can tell him that for me."

You can tell him that yourself. That's what Dave wanted to say, but he didn't say it.

160

Max's tone became contemptuous. "Looks like you're on the other side of the fence now Dave, workin' for that rich snob Walden."

"He's not a rich snob," Dave mumbled.

Max pretended not to hear, "Yup, you're on the other side of the fence now, Dave." Max's voice was rich with scorn. "Law and order. Obey all the traffic rules like a good little boy. Put your hand out when you make a turn; stop at all the stop signs; don't exceed the speed limit. Humph." Max gave a snort of contempt.

Just then the front door opened and a female voice said, "Is that you, Dave?"

"I've got to go," Dave said.

Max stepped close, spoke low and harshly. "Listen Dave, get wise to yourself. Don't sell out to Currie and Walden. They're out to break up our gang, d'y' realize that? They hate hot rods and everything about 'em. We got t' stick together, Dave, understand?"

"I suppose so," Dave mumbled.

His mother's voice cut sharply across the front porch. "Dave, who are you talking to out there?"

"Listen, Dave," Max clutched Dave by the collar of his leather jacket. The voice rasped, "Know what I'm going to do for you, fella? I'm going to get the gang to take up a collection, each of us chip in a couple of bucks apiece—pay your fine. How about that?"

"Dave." His mother's voice was angry now.

"I gotta go." Dave tried to pull away.

"O.K." Max suddenly released his grip, knocking Dave slightly off balance. "But you're still on our side, Dave, whether you like it or not. And don't forget it."

"G'night," Dave mumbled. He hurried over the lawn, stumbled up the front steps, glanced over his shoulder; Max had disappeared in the darkness.

But Dave's mother was suspicious. "Who was that, Dave? Did he have to be so mysterious?"

"Oh, it was just a guy who—"

The raucous defiant blast of a motorcycle severed the sentence.

His mother bristled. "I know who that was. It was Max Werner. Dave," his mother's eyes blinked angrily, "I think you've seen just about enough of that trouble maker."

"I didn't ask him over," Dave mumbled.

"Well, see that you never do," said his mother sharply. "And now take off that terrible jacket and cap and sit down to your supper."

Dave's fear and confusion fused into defiance, "What's wrong with my jacket and cap?"

"The main thing wrong with them," said his mother sharply, "is that they remind me of a very objectionable young man named Max Werner."

"Criticism," Dave mumbled, "seems to be all I get these days."

162

"What's that?" said his mother sharply.

"Nothing," said Dave, hanging up his cap and jacket. Not even mumbling seemed safe any more. He would have to talk to himself. Which he did as he ate his supper. He talked to himself mainly about his Model A. When would he ever get a chance to replace that head gasket, fix that wobble in the front wheel? Perhaps Mr. Walden would let him have Saturday afternoon off.

At almost that very moment Webb Walden was arriving home in his jeep. As he was about to enter the house his ears picked up the sound of an unusually powerful engine; it sounded like the Ford-Duesenberg. Was Angus road testing it at this time of night?

The sound of the engine increased, then revved up, *arroomm*; with a roar the Ford-Duesenberg rolled into the driveway.

Grinning, Webb flagged it to a stop. "Hi Angus, practicing for the Branchville hill climb?"

Angus poked his head out of the cockpit, "How's that again? A hill climb right here in Branchville? Are ye out of your mind, lad?"

Webb laughed. "I wouldn't be surprised. But that's beside the point. Come on in and eat supper with me and I'll tell you all the news."

"All rright," said Angus and his voice suddenly be-

163

came ominous. "And I'll give you some news of my own."

Webb caught the ominous tone. "What's the matter, Angus, any trouble with the apprentice?"

"A great deal," said Angus darkly.

Webb frowned. Doubt and worry plucked at him like dirty beggar's fingers and he tried without success to brush them off. He was tired, hungry. He had covered a good deal of ground, talked to many people about many problems; now, before supper, was no time to hear about a troublesome apprentice—let that headache wait at least until after hunger was satisfied.

It was satisfied so voraciously that Webb's wife snorted and said, "The only difference between you two men and the big cats in the zoo at feeding time is that the big cats are prettier and have valuable coats. Which reminds me, Webb. I'll be needing a new spring coat for Easter."

Webb wiped his mouth and sighed, "Ah, you're a wonderful cook, dear. You can make meatballs and spaghetti taste just like sirloin steak and French fried potatoes."

"You're lucky to get meatballs and spaghetti," snapped Hortense.

Webb smiled benevolently. "Don't get me wrong. My remark wasn't a complaint, it was a compliment."

"Forget it," said Hortense. "Tell me what you accomplished today. Did you talk to Max Werner?"

"I did," said Webb. "A foul ball, a teen-age twerp, and the real ringleader of the Milltown hot rods. Our friend Dave was just the sucker who took a 'bum rap' as they say in criminal circles."

"That's what I thought," said Hortense. "Then you saw Constable Currie?"

"I did," said Webb. "Had a pleasant talk with the constable. He's very grateful to me for souping up his car."

"Is that all?"

"Nope. The constable is also going to have a chat with Max Werner. The constable will prepare his own report on the case and turn it over to the prosecuting attorney. You underrate these people, dear; Constable Currie and Amos Sefton have a lot more common sense than you think."

"That's what you keep telling me," snapped his wife.

"Constable Currie is very cooperative," said Webb. "In fact I'm willing to bet that we put on a hill climb right here in Branchville."

"Really, Webb?" Hortense was genuinely surprised.

"Really and truly," grinned Webb, "for three good reasons."

"What are they?"

"Constable Currie will keep the course clear. To do that he'll need four or five deputies. That will make Currie chief of police, something he's always wanted to be. Reason number two—the local merchants will benefit because the hill climb will attract a big crowd. And reason number three, Hortense, is right up your alley."

"How come?" asked Hortense.

"The P.T.A.," said Webb. "It should sponsor something like this."

"You're crazy," said Hortense flatly.

Webb grinned. "Maybe I am. Nevertheless it's a good cause for the P.T.A."

"I don't see how," said Hortense. "To most members of the P.T.A. a hot rod is a device of the devil."

"It doesn't have to be," said Webb. He drank his coffee and continued calmly. "We might as well face it—hot rods are here to stay, whether we like them or not. They're junior sports cars—that's what they are. And like sports cars they represent a healthy interest in the peak performance of automobile engines."

"But what about the traffic laws they break," said Hortense. "Is that healthy?"

"Of course not," said Webb, "but that's just part of the picture. Figure it this way: nine-tenths of the time a boy like Dave Neil has an absorbing and useful hobby—working on automobile engines. But in one-tenth of that time he breaks traffic laws. So what? So our job is to change that law-breaking one-tenth into something legal like a Sports Car Club competition, a hill climb for example."

"That sounds like something worth while," said

Hortense, "but P.T.A. mothers will say, 'Isn't a hill climb dangerous?' "

"Isn't football dangerous?" Webb countered. "Players break legs, necks, collarbones. It doesn't stop football, it doesn't bother the players, for they're heroes. But some boys like Dave Neil and Max Werner aren't much good at sports and they feel left out. So they show their ability in another field—auto engines. They work hard and they often work well. Unfortunately they sometimes spoil everything as Dave Neil did, by trying to be a hero on the wrong side of the fence. What we should do is to show boys like Dave how to stay on the right side of the fence."

Webb finished his coffee, leaned back, smiled at his wife, "Do I sound sensible for a change? Can you sell this to the P.T.A.? You'll make money on parking lots and programs. You'll probably make enough to buy that playground equipment the school needs. And incidentally—" Webb leaned forward again—"with the money earned at the hill climb, we could buy the school a simple engine like a Model A and show kids how it works—how to put one together, how to repair it. Couldn't we, Angus?" Webb grinned and tapped his assistant lightly on the back.

"Ach," said Angus.

"We might even have a weekly class in safe driving," said Webb. He chuckled. "Angus, wouldn't you like to give driving lessons to pretty girl students? I can

167

hear them now." Webb turned his deep voice falsetto, "Oh, Professor MacKenzie, please, sir, would you explain the difference between peeling rubber and breaking traction?"

"Ugh," said Angus.

Hortense laughed. "Webb, you're really steamed up about this, aren't you? And what amuses me is that you got into it so reluctantly."

"I don't remember being reluctant," said Webb indignantly.

"Of course you don't," said Hortense and, still smiling, she turned to Angus MacKenzie. "What's the matter with you, Angus, cat got your tongue?"

"I'm thinking about a grave problem that's coom up," burred Angus, packing tobacco into an ancient pipe.

"If you're going to smoke that thing," said Hortense, "I'm getting out of here."

"Wait 'til you hear the rest of the day's news," said Webb. He smiled at them triumphantly and raised his voice. "I located a Model J!"

"Good," said Hortense, genuinely pleased.

"Ach," said Angus, packing his pipe.

"It's in Cliffwood, New Jersey," Webb explained, "and I heard it's owned by a young man named Courtney Cavendish."

"Ach," said Angus again.

"Goodness," said Hortense. And then in a voice

suddenly suspicious she asked, "Who told you about the Model J, Webb?"

"Lucky Louie," said Webb casually.

"That bandit!" cried Hortense. "What did you buy from Lucky Louie that unlocked his unscrupulous tongue?"

"Oh, some Duesenberg parts," said Webb in an off-hand way.

"Many?" said Hortense, with a sharp intake of breath.

"I got a bargain," Webb protested.

"Heaven help us!" said Hortense.

"Ach," said Angus.

"How much?" asked Hortense icily.

"Only a thousand dollars," said Webb defensively.

Hortense cried, "Webb Walden! You raving lunatic!"

Angus moaned, "A thousand dollars? Ach mon, you've drained the ruddy till."

Hortense continued, "There goes my Easter coat, a new vacuum cleaner, a washing machine!"

"Now just a minute," said Webb indignantly, "think of it this way. Ten small deals with Lucky Louie might cost me fifteen hundred dollars, but one deal involving the same amount of equipment cost me only a thousand. So I saved five hundred."

"At that rrate," burred Angus, "you should be secrretarry of the trreasurry. A brrain like yours is wasted in the sporrts carr business."

"It certainly is," cried Hortense, noisily piling up the dishes. "It should be in a medical museum." She stomped out of the dining room.

Webb smiled sadly. "Ah women, they just don't seem to understand the sports car business—do they, Angus?"

"Does anybody?" asked Angus, lighting his pipe.

"Now, Angus," Webb chided, "think of the thrrill you get when our Ford-Duesenberg wins a hill climb or road race."

"Ach," said Angus, "I get a bigger thrrill when we sell something for a prrofit. We're a thousand dollars in the hole now, mon. So we'll have to sell the phaeton. Take it down to Jersey with you and palm it off on that lunatic Courtney Cavendish."

Webb grinned, "How d'y' know Courtney is a lunatic?"

"All car collectors are crazy," said Angus, puffing on his pipe. "Take me advice, mon, and sell that phaeton to Cavendish when you buy his Model J; and don't take a penny less than twenty-five hundred for it. For the phaeton is in fine shape, y'know. And the Model J is probably a mess."

Angus disappeared for a moment behind a cloud of pipe smoke but his Scottish accents rolled through, "Now tell me, mon, while we're on life's most int'resting soobject—money—what are we paying this apprentice?"

"Seventy-five cents an hour," said Webb.

Angus groaned. "That's a terribly high wage. Why the lad should be paying us for the education he's getting."

Webb laughed. "Maybe. But it seems to me that there's some kind of minimum wage law in this state."

"Ach, it's terrible what we've come to," said Angus, emerging from a cloud of smoke. "We not only have to teach these brrats but we have to pay them—and him sooch a prroblem lad at that."

"Is he?" said Webb, suddenly anxious. "Didn't he do the dirty work? Didn't he fix the flats, Angus?"

"Aye, he fixed the flats," said Angus puffing.

"Charge the batteries?"

"He charrged the batteries," said Angus.

"Flush the radiator?"

"He flooshed the radiator."

"Well then"—Webb was smiling triumphantly—"how is he such a problem? Does he swear, steal, spit on the floor?"

"Naaa," said Angus, puffing furiously on his pipe. "It's a different type of prroblem. This lad is soofferring from a grrave mental disease."

"How do you know?" said Webb sharply. "I suppose you tapped his knee with a ball-peen hammer?"

"Ach no," said Angus. "I wouldn't tap his knee—it's

171

his head that needs the tap. This lad is all knotted up mentally." Angus puffed up a big cloud of smoke and spoke through it, "Y'know, Webb, there are one hundred different varieties of lunatics at larrge in this daft worrld we inhabit and, of the one hundred, I have had close acquaintance with three types."

"Which three?" said Webb.

"Well," said Angus, emerging from the smoke, "firrst of all there are the car collectors like Courtney Cavendish; secondly there are the followers of the Brooklyn Dodgers—"

"And thirdly?" said Webb.

Angus puffed. "The thirrd varriety," he said, "claims our friend the apprentice." He leaned back, blew all the smoke away, and, speaking vehemently, said, "Ye know what, mon? The worrst possible varriety of lunacy has afflicted our friend the apprrentice—he's a Yankee fan, a rooter for the arroostoocrrats, a worrshipper of that upstarrt Mickey Mantle."

"Hoot mon!" cried Webb laughing, "the monster of Loch Ness is on the loose again!"

Angus sputtered indignantly over his pipe. "Marrk my worrds, mon, a Yankee fan is ten times more of a menace than the poor auld monster of Loch Ness."

"Aw—" Webb began.

"Ach," Angus began, and Webb's wife marched in with plates of pie. "What's all the noise about?"

"The apprentice," laughed Webb. "Angus has found a brother under the skin, a Yankee fan."

"But I'm for the Giants!" Angus protested angrily.

"Oh," said Hortense innocently, "and all this time I thought you were for the Dodgers."

"Hoot mon!" cried Webb, roaring with laughter. "Isn't anybody for the Chicago Cubs? Anyway, I'm taking the apprentice with me to New Jersey on Saturday. I'll probably need someone who's good at fixing flats."

"What you need," said Hortense, "is a padlock on your wallet."

"Ach," said Angus, "ye can say that again."

Chapter XV

SATURDAY afternoon off. That's what Dave wanted so that he could work on his Model A. He had made the superficial repairs on fender and bumper. Now he wanted to tackle the serious work on the head gasket and the wobble in the wheel. If any member of the Milltown Hot Rod Club had told Dave he would spend Saturday in New Jersey tracking down a Model J Duesenberg he would have said, "Who me? Not on your life."

But something happened on Friday that firmed Dave's fluctuating attitude. For on Friday afternoon Dave worked on a sports car engine with Webb Walden.

First of all the carburetors were cleaned, not one

or two but four big special racing carburetors. And, as they worked on the carburetors, Webb said, "Dave, didn't your Model A have dual exhausts and only one carburetor?"

Dave admitted it, adding, "But twin pipes cut down on the back pressure."

"Sure," Webb agreed. "But it would be a fairly simple matter to put in another carburetor and a special manifold. There are a couple of Winfields around here that I could let you have at cost."

"Winfields?" said Dave.

Webb smiled. "A bigger and better carb than the one you have now, Dave. Also, I noticed that your solitary Model A carb is an updraft job under the engine block. We could fit the Winfields on above the block and have gravity flow instead of updraft; in other words, less effort for the engine to get its fuel."

Wow, said Dave, but he said it to himself. Two carbs—Winfields, bigger, better. And placed in a position for gravity flow instead of updraft. Gosh, if the Model A ever spent a week in this shop it would come out so hot it would make Max Werner's V-8 look like a kiddy car.

Later, the work on the sports car engine turned the talk to pistons, domed pistons.

"Why are they domed?" Dave wanted to know.

"To increase the compression ratio," said Webb

175

Walden. "Those domed pistons come round, semi-finished. We cam grind them."

"Cam grind them?" Dave asked.

"Yes, you know how the camshaft works. A cam or lobe is used on a machine that grinds the piston, making its shape oval instead of round. Cam-ground aluminum pistons fit better in the steel cylinders because their oval shape allows them to expand under terrific heat without seizing the wall of the cylinder." Webb chuckled. "You can imagine how embarrassing that would be to a driver tearing around Watkins Glen at 120 miles an hour."

"Jeepers." Dave was so carried away by the theory of cam-ground pistons that he was appalled by the possibilities of a seized cylinder. Gradually coming down to earth, he asked, "How about domed pistons for my Model A, Mr. Walden?"

Webb smiled. "What we could do, Dave, would be to give your Model A a high-compression head using the same studs and water pump. That would give you a higher compression ratio, say eight to one instead of four to one."

Holy smoke. Dave was dizzy with delight. Racing along the road in his Model A, Dave had often felt intoxicated with sensations of speed and power. But this was the first time he had ever felt that way standing still in a workshop. And he knew why. He had been taken into a different world, the world of the master mechanic working on high-speed engines. And the contrast with Max Werner and the hot rod club was shattering—to Max Werner and the club.

But Dave did not let his intoxication obliterate the fact that his Model A was crippled. It was all very well to talk about high-compression heads and Winfield carburetors but how about the head gasket and the wobble in the wheel?

"Oh that," said Webb as if discussing something as simple as a dead battery, "just bring your Model A over on Sunday afternoon, Dave, and we'll take care of those minor matters."

Minor matters? Dave gulped. Head gasket, wheel wobble, minor matters? Well, he supposed they were —to a master mechanic working with high-compression heads and cam-ground domed pistons. In any case Dave was delighted at the prospect of getting expert help on the Model A on Sunday. So when Mr. Walden brought up the subject of Saturday's trip to New Jersey, Dave was all enthusiasm.

And this enthusiasm had an interesting side effect. After work that Friday, Webb drove Dave home in the jeep. On the way Webb stopped at the Branchville shopping center for one of his close-cropped haircuts. Dave suddenly decided that he would get one too, just like Mr. Walden's. The crew cut made the sideburns look even sillier, so off they came with two strokes of the barber's straight razor. The next thing to come off was the hot rodder's peaked cap, for without a bushy head of hair to support it the cap fell down over Dave's ears. Dave didn't care. He stared at himself in the barbershop mirror and said, "Boy, I sure look different."

"Boy, you sure do," said Mr. Walden smiling.

"Wonder what Ma will think?"

Mr. Walden chuckled. "She'll probably think it's a great improvement."

She did.

At seven o'clock the next morning Dave bounced out of bed, brushed his teeth, stared at himself in the mirror. It was still a startling sight. Gone but unlamented was the untamed bushy hair, the long tapering sideburns. Dave grinned at the new face and ran one hand over his crew cut. Gosh, it felt just like a soft brush. It was clean, neat—and it would never have to be combed. Dave's grin turned into a laugh. He whistled as he put on sport shirt, sport coat, slacks.

It was a soft spring day. There was no school and he was going to New Jersey on a Duesenberg hunt. He looked in the mirror again, straightened his shoulders. Not bad. An improvement, definitely. Still whistling, Dave skipped downstairs to the kitchen. "Hi Ma, breakfast ready?"

"Almost. Hungry, son?"

"Very," he said.

After breakfast he wandered restlessly around the small house.

"Make your bed, Dave," said his mother.

"Do I have time?" he parried.

"Of course you have time," she said. "It's only quarter of eight."

He bounded upstairs, thinking, I can remember when Ma would make my bed for me—not so long ago either. But not any more.

Bed made, he ran downstairs to the kitchen again. "Mr. Walden here yet?"

"No, Dave." His mother smiled. "Give him a chance, it's only five of eight."

"Oh," said Dave.

"Why don't you dry the breakfast dishes while you're waiting?"

He sighed but said, "O.K. Better take off my jacket." He took off the coat, hung it carefully on the back of a chair. "What are you smiling at, Ma?" He brushed a hand over his head. "Don't you like my crew cut?"

She turned from the kitchen sink and said in a firm voice, "I think it's the best haircut you ever had in your life."

He grinned. "I kind of like it myself."

She smiled. "I guess you're getting to like Mr. Walden, aren't you?"

Dave shrugged his shoulders. "Oh, he's all right."

A horn sounded out front.

179

"There he is!" cried Dave. He grabbed his coat and ran shouting, "So long, Ma!"

"So long, son." Mrs. Neil was smiling happily, but behind her glasses her eyes were blinking much faster than usual.

Webb Walden led the way to New Jersey in the Duesenberg phaeton. Dave followed in the jeep and got a lesson in "pleasure" driving. Signs that Dave had once disregarded now assumed special significance. And somehow they didn't seem annoying any more but sensible guides to good driving. They must be, Dave thought, for wasn't Mr. Walden obeying them all to the letter? He was. He was stopping at the stop signs, obeying the speed limits, giving clear hand signals for left and right turns. All this, though Mr. Walden was at the wheel of a high-powered car which could outdistance even the state troopers. In other words Mr. Walden had plenty of power but he didn't abuse it. How different, thought Dave, from the Milltown Hot Rod Club.

They drove along the Merritt Parkway at fifty-five miles an hour. That was fast enough. They drove onto the island of Manhattan over a double-decker bridge at a dizzy height above a sparkling estuary called Spuyten Duyvil. The scenery was spectacular. Far below to the right ran the broad blue waters of the Hudson. Across the great river, high cliffs rose precipitously, the New Jersey Palisades.

Down they rolled along the Henry Hudson Parkway, a fast six-lane dual highway, then up they circled to the magnificent George Washington bridge, breathtakingly high over the Hudson. Crossing the bridge with magnificent views to left and right, they drove onto the New Jersey Turnpike and sped to their destination at sixty miles an hour.

The ride was a revelation to Dave. Here was a magnificent network of roads connecting Connecticut, New York, and New Jersey. The legal speed limits for this highway network provided fast passage with as much safety as science could produce. Then wasn't it sensible to drive within the speed limits and obey the reasonable signs along the highways, saving the super speed and spectacular driving for specially supervised hill climbs and road races?

That's the question Webb Walden's exemplary driving seemed to ask as it guided Dave along the parkways of three states. And the answer Dave gave was exactly the opposite to the defiant chip-on-the-shoulder reply he would once have given as a member of the Milltown Hot Rod Club.

Right turn coming. Webb Walden's left arm was signaling, hand up, palm forward. Following the signal, Dave turned off the turnpike and headed for Cliffwood and the home of Courtney Cavendish.

And what a home it was. A forbidding stone wall surrounded a tremendous red brick house with white columns that dominated a swimming pool, a tennis court and two garages, one tremendous, the other just a six-car affair. As the jeep and the phaeton were parked on the street, Dave noticed a sign that said "Service Entrance" and smiled at the memory the sign revived; this was the way he had once pictured the home of Webb Walden—how different the home and its owner had turned out to be!

But as for Courtney Cavendish—he was just about what Dave had imagined. Courtney was a cherub. He had a soft, round face elegantly decorated with a thin mustache and a long cigarette holder. In fact, "elegant" was the word for Courtney Cavendish. It showed in his appearance and in his taste for automobiles. They were all elegant, from a Daniels Town Brougham to a Jordan Sport Marine. It wasn't what was under the hood that interested Courtney, it was the body of the car and its extras. Courtney Cavendish reminded Dave of those automobile salesmen who gush over the radios, cigarette lighters, and ventilation systems and skip over the performance of the engine.

With a wave of his cigarette at the Jordan Sport Marine, Mr. Cavendish said, "Notice the tonneau light, empaneled in Honduran mahogany."

Dave ignored the Honduran mahogany and stared at a racy coupe that vaguely reminded him of his crippled Model A. He said as much and was rewarded with a withering look and a scornful comment from Courtney Cavendish: "That, my dear boy, is like comparing a bracelet from Woolworth's with a necklace from Tiffany's. You happen to be looking at a custom-built Kissel Six."

"Oh," said Dave. He felt embarrassed until he saw Webb Walden wink as if to say, Don't mind him, his nursemaid dropped him on his head.

Aloud Webb said, "Do you work on these cars yourself, Mr. Cavendish?"

"Uh, well, not as much as I used to," said Cavendish. He deftly pushed a cigarette into the long holder, lit it, inhaled deeply, exhaled proudly. "Before the cost of living caught up with us, our chauffeur Jenkins put my cars in shape; a marvelous grease monkey, Jenkins. I miss him terribly." Chauncey sighed. "Now I have to depend on mother's gardener and at this time of the year he's so involved with his blessed plants and transplants that he has no time for the finer things of life." Mr. Cavendish sighed with a thick shaft of smoke, *"C'est la vie."*

"Absolutely," said Webb with another wink at Dave.

Diverting the guided tour to an open door, Mr. Cavendish waved his cigarette holder at the smaller garage and said, "There's an example of what I'm up against. There are six hulks sitting over there dying of neglect."

"May we look at them?" asked Webb Walden.

"Certainly," said Cavendish, "but, my dear fellow, I can assure you that they are not a very edifying spectacle—you won't possibly be able to imagine what they will look like when they're fixed up."

Oh no? said Dave to himself. That happens to be our specialty, Mr. Walden's and mine.

The hulks were covered with canvas and again Dave's memory flipped back into the past, this time to the scene in his barn when he proudly unveiled his Model A to the members of the Milltown Hot Rod Club. But there was no pride in Courtney Cavendish as he pulled at a canvas and uncovered a car called a Pierce Arrow. He was disinterested; so were Dave and Webb Walden. Another canvas, another car; an ancient Cunningham limousine. Webb showed some interest in this, contrasting it with the Cunningham sports car of 1953. Cavendish ignored him and, yanking at a third canvas, said, "Duesenberg."

Duesenberg! Dave twitched like a startled rabbit. He noticed however that Webb Walden was calm. "What year?" Webb was asking in a matter-of-fact tone.

"I haven't the slightest idea," said Chauncey. "All I know is that it has a chronograph."

"What's that?" Dave asked.

"A split-second stop clock," said Cavendish condescendingly. "It is curiosities like chronographs, small but significant, that make car collecting worth while. They compensate for the headaches. Take this Duesy, for example. I had a terrible time getting its fuel pump to work."

"I see," said Webb Walden easily. "Mind if I take a look?"

"Not at all," said Courtney Cavendish.

Dave listened, watched, wondered. What was Webb going to do? Was there a motive behind all this? There must be.

With Dave at his elbow Webb Walden examined the Duesenberg's gas pump and said, "Quite a pump. Special aircraft type—bronze bellows and all. But whoever tried to install it broke the housing."

"Oh goodness!" said Cavendish. "Defective housing, eh? Awfully sloppy workmanship on parts these days."

Sloppy workmanship my eye, said Dave to himself. I'll bet it was Courtney himself who did the sloppy work and broke the housing.

"Mechanical details have always bored me," said Cavendish, flipping an ash from his cigarette. "I have always tried to look at the big picture, the finished product, the whole work of art." He cleared his throat. "As a matter of fact I just happen to have another fuel pump and if you'd care to, uh, experiment, I mean, uh—"

"Get this Model J to run?" said Webb with a grin. "Maybe I could. But Mr. Cavendish, wouldn't you rather have a Duesenberg that's all shined up and ready to roll?"

"Naturally," he answered. "But where on earth will I find such a car?"

185

"On the other side of your stone wall," said Webb calmly.

"No!" cried Courtney Cavendish. "A Duesenberg all tuned up and ready to roll. What kind of a Dusey, may I ask?"

"A phaeton," said Webb.

"A phaeton!" Cavendish was ecstatic. "Lead me to it!"

"Gladly," said Webb.

Holy crow, said Dave to himself. Mrs. Walden is going to get her Easter coat.

It certainly looked that way. Mr. Cavendish was delighted with the phaeton and considered its price reasonable after deducting three hundred dollars for the Model J which he seemed glad to trade in on a finished product. A bill of sale was made out, a check signed, and in these clerical operations Courtney Cavendish was elegantly efficient as he stamped the bill of sale and signed a check with the most illegible signature Dave had ever seen.

This done, Mr. Cavendish went off to lunch, leaving Dave and Webb Walden working on the Model J with equipment taken from the jeep. And once again Dave found himself admiring Webb Walden's mechanical ability. Not only did Webb quickly install the new fuel pump but in a short space of time he dismantled the distributor and cleaned and adjusted its points while

Dave attended to simpler things like spark plugs, battery, tires, and finally, oil, gas, and water.

Then Webb Walden slid behind the Model J's wheel and with a grin said, "Ready? Contact!"

Aruruh-ruruh—ROAR. The engine exploded and Dave let out a cheer that was lost in the wonderful sound of the Model J coming to life.

Slowly, carefully, Webb Walden guided the big car out of the garage. Safe from fumes of carbon monoxide he examined the engine again and said, "It's only running on four cylinders out of eight but it's running. We'll make it, Dave, don't worry." Webb grinned. "Which car do you want to drive back to Connecticut, the Duesy or the jeep?"

"The Duesy," said Dave without a moment's hesitation.

"That's the spirit," said Webb. "Some day, Dave, you'll drive this Duesy—the racing car we make out of it—in a Sports Car Club hill climb."

"Will I, Mr. Walden?" Dave was exuberant. So many wonderful things had happened so fast. The Model J had been found, purchased. It was going to be streamlined, souped up into a racing car. And he Dave Neil, was going to be allowed to drive it.

Webb smiled. "But don't be impatient, Dave. It'll take time and work, plenty of both, a lot of work on the car in the shop and a lot of work behind the wheel on the road."

"That's O.K. by me," said Dave smiling.

"Good," said Webb. His smile widened. "By now I guess you can see how many angles there are to this sports car business. You have to be a good grease monkey, a Yankee trader, a good judge of engines as well as human beings, a driver who won't lose his nerve at a speed of 125 miles an hour on an ordinary road and—" Webb laughed—"last but not least, a person with a great deal of patience.

"Meanwhile," Webb tapped Dave on the shoulder, "you drive the jeep and I'll drive the Duesy. It's a pretty sick car as it stands and I'd better be at the controls."

They drove slowly down the driveway, the Duesenberg in the lead, the jeep close behind. Suddenly, as they came abreast of the red brick house, it happened; Courtney Cavendish dashed out from under the white columns crying, "Wait! Wait!"

"For what?" Dave asked. "Does Courtney want a ride up to Connecticut?"

No. Courtney wanted his chronograph, the split-second stop clock on the Duesy's dashboard. But Webb wouldn't give it to him. And as Dave watched, fascinated, Courtney Cavendish stamped his feet, chewed his mustache, and cried, "If you don't give me back my chronograph I'll call the police and have you arrested!"

Was he out of his mind? Could collectors be so

crazy about chronographs? Apparently they could for the man was throwing a tantrum. But it had no effect on Webb Walden. His voice was unruffled as he said, "Listen, Cavendish, that's not your chronograph, it's mine. It became mine when we swapped cars."

"I didn't sell you my chronograph," cried Cavendish. "I just sold you the Model J!"

"Okay," said Webb calmly, "I didn't sell you the tachometer on the dashboard of the phaeton. If you start stripping the Model J of its accessories I'll do the same with the phaeton."

This logic deflated Courtney. It was as if the string choking the neck of a balloon had suddenly been cut, releasing all the hot air in a sputtery blast that blew the balloon hither and yon in a fantastic fading flight. Courtney Cavendish almost took off. He fumed, he jumped up and down—and he subsided just as a tall regal woman emerged from the house and announced in an imperious voice, "I am Mrs. Cavendish and I should like to know what in the name of heaven is going on out here."

Webb Walden introduced himself and explained the argument, producing the bill of sale to back up his story.

"So that's it," said Mrs. Cavendish, handing back the bill of sale as if disposing of a piece of Limburger cheese. And then she spoke to her son, "Courtney, you signed a gentleman's agreement and you must abide by it."

"But he's no gentleman," said Courtney, pointing at Webb from a safe distance.

"Whether he is or not is immaterial," said Mrs. Cavendish coldly. "When a son of mine signs an agreement he carries it out. Personally, son, I think you were most fortunate to get rid of that old wreck with or without its crabblegraph. Let us consider the matter settled." Mrs. Cavendish turned from her son to Webb Walden and with her head even higher said, "Good day, Mr. Weller." And she disappeared into the house.

Dave was dazed. Mrs. Cavendish was some character even if she did call a chronograph a crabble-graph, Mr. Walden Mr. Weller, and the Model J an old wreck. She was a character just the same—and she *had* character—which was more than could be said for her son, who was stomping off with a sullen look on his cherubic face while little clouds of smoke belched petulantly from his cigarette holder.

Webb was chuckling, "Well, it's easy to see who wears the pants in that family. Poor Courtney."

Poor Courtney? Dave asked himself as he slowly followed the Duesenberg in the jeep. Why poor Courtney? He had everything served up on a silver platter. But was that good? Look how he turned out. He couldn't install a fuel pump, clean a carburetor, adjust the points on a distributor—why, he'd get his hands

190

dirty. He couldn't even conclude an argument about a chronograph. "Poor Courtney" was right; he didn't have a chance; his mother wouldn't give him one.

All this led Dave to a review of his own domestic relations. And he candidly asked himself, Was I ever a mother's boy? It was a startling question and he answered it as truthfully as possible: I guess Ma did let me get away with some things. I guess it wasn't easy for her to keep me in line. I didn't cooperate very much. Ma was right all the time but I just wouldn't listen. She was right when she said I needed man-to-man talks although I thought at the time that she was just being corny. But she was right about that. And she was certainly right about Max Werner.

Chapter XVI

THE very night that Dave returned from New Jersey he had an opportunity to turn theory into action. First of all Dave dried the supper dishes without being asked. And secondly—

Bbbrrraaattt. A blast from a motorcycle almost made Dave drop a wet dish on the kitchen floor. As he caught it he glanced up and saw his mother's eyes blinking nervously behind her spectacles.

"You know who that is," she said.

"I know," said Dave.

"I don't want you to have anything more to do with him."

"I think I'd better talk to him," Dave said. He put down the dish he had dried, hung up the towel. He was surprised by his own calmness and determination.

"Dave," said his mother nervously.

He took a deep breath, swallowed hard. "I'll handle this," he said and walked out through the kitchen door. There were butterflies in his stomach but his head was high, his shoulders erect, his fists clenched.

"Dave," his mother called after him in a high, thin voice.

"Hi, Dave." Max's voice came from the opposite direction. It was neither high nor thin. It was more hoarsely belligerent than ever. A shaft of light from the kitchen fell on Max's cap cocked at a jaunty angle, the sideburns, the leather jacket, the flashy belt with the red and green reflectors.

"Hi," said Dave coolly and he said to himself, Gosh, Max looks silly. And to think that I once thought he looked sharp and tried to imitate him. Holy smoke!

"Everything's all set," said Max boastfully.

"How do you mean?" said Dave.

Max hooked his thumbs in his fancy belt, "I've got my hot rod running again, Dave. The old V-8 is all ready for that hill climb your new pal is gonna put on over in Branchville. I heard all about it yesterday."

Dave stared, stricken. "You mean it's official— they're really going to run that hill climb?"

"Sure," said Max. "Know who told me? Chet Coley. His filling station is gonna be the place where they inspect the cars."

193

"Chet Coley told you?" said Dave. All he could do was to echo the words stupidly in a stunned voice.

"Sure. Constable Currie told Chet and Chet told me," boasted Max. "So I'm entering my hot rod. And know what, Dave boy? I'm gonna win that hill climb."

Win the hill climb—Max Werner? Sure, that's what he said. Max wasn't going to challenge Constable Currie; oh no, not Max; he wouldn't stick his neck out, he'd let someone else do it, some sucker like me, Dave told himself. Max and his lousy V-8 will compete in a legal hill climb but I won't be able to drive my Model A in it because my license will be suspended.

Anger welled up in Dave. And as it rushed up through him it stopped the fluttering of the butter-flies, set his jaw, clenched his fists so hard that the fingernails dug into palms.

"What about the money?" he asked in a voice that shook with emotion.

"What money?" said Max feigning innocence.

"The money you were going to collect and put up for my fine," said Dave, his voice shaking.

"Oh," said Max carelessly. "Well, uh, that's been sort of tough sleddin' Dave. Everybody seems to be busted, includin' me. But gee, Dave," Max's voice rose confidently, "everything else has sure worked out swell. Why, we got those people in Branchville comin' and goin'. You led 'em a merry chase in your Model A,

Dave, and now me and my V-8'll show that rich snob Webb Walden—"

Smack. Dave hit Max right on the nose.

Max staggered back, clapped his hand to his face, gasping, swearing. He stumbled and sat down and from his ignominious sitting position he bleated "It's bleedin'."

Dave stared at the spectacle. He couldn't believe his eyes. But he knew from the pain in the knuckles of his right hand that it had happened; he had smacked Max. His hand hurt. But that didn't matter. What mattered was that Max, the loud mouthed, double-crossing leader of the Milltown Hot Rod Club had been knocked on his backside. His peaked cap had come off, revealing ridiculously long hair that tapered into those silly sideburns. But not just the sideburns were silly. Did Max realize how ridiculous he looked sitting there on the ground holding onto his nose, bleating like a sheep? Apparently he did because he salvaged some of his pride, turned his bleat into a snarl, scrambled up, and charged.

Bracing himself for the onslaught, Dave managed to stay on his feet. Though wild blows landed on his head, shoulder, and ribs, he fought back furiously right, left, left, right. Max rushed in head down, butted Dave in the stomach, tripped him up, knocked him down. Crunch. For the first time one of Max's wild swings really connected near Dave's right eye. It hurt,

195

it stunned, it sent white stars flashing. But Dave still fought back, his anger wiping away the pain—it was just like Max to butt and trip, then hit you when you were down. Fiercely Dave struggled free, scrambled up, raised his fists, lashed out with them. His right eye ached, his right fist throbbed but he was ready and determined to continue.

He watched Max get up slowly, wiping his bleeding nose, breathing heavily. Max was winded; all those cigarettes he smoked in his show-off way were beginning to take their toll. Could he go on?

"Break it up, boys," said a gruff voice.

A tall, stout figure emerged from the semidarkness. It was Mr. Miller, the Neil's next-door neighbor. He had evidently heard the noise of the fight and taken upon himself the role of a neutral but determined peacemaker. Then he recognized Max Werner and his voice lost its neutrality. "Oh, so it's you. I might have known. Now you take yourself and that blasted motorcycle out of here."

"Oh yeah?" There was a little defiance left in Max's voice. "Who's gonna make me?"

"We are," said Mr. Miller. "Come on, Dave!"

"Two against one!" squawked Max and ran for his motorcycle.

Mr. Miller gave a grunt of disdain and then asked, "You all right, Dave?"

Dave's head ached, his knuckles throbbed, but he

said, "Sure I'm all right." He listened to the motor-cycle blat into action, roar away.

"Good riddance to bad rubbish," said Mr. Miller. "The nerve of that twerp. Not only makes too much noise but starts fights."

"He didn't start it," said Dave, proudly, "I did."

"Well, good for you!" said Mr. Miller, his gruff voice rising with surprise. "About time somebody popped that brat on the nose. Oh, good evening, Mrs. Neil."

Dave swung around. There was his mother. And why in heaven's name was she wrestling with that mop?

Mrs. Neil laughed nervously and in a voice quickened by relief said, "I didn't want to interfere, Mr. Miller, but when that boy Max tripped up my son Dave and hit him when he was down I saw red and grabbed my mop." She laughed. "Then I realized it was too soft to hit that pest with so I unscrewed the handle so I'd be sure and hit him with something he'd notice."

Mr. Miller laughed but Dave said indignantly. "Gosh Ma, you don't have to do things like that. I told you I could handle Max."

"I know," said his mother, "but I wasn't quite sure. I mean—" She started to explain, then stopped and changed the subject.

Neither was I sure, Dave admitted to himself. Not so long ago I wouldn't have been able to handle Max

Werner. But things have changed since I met a man named Webb Walden.

Webb Walden had just finished the dessert to his Sunday dinner when Dave showed up. Webb wiped his mouth and sighed. "Ah, there's nothing like apple pie à la mode. I think I even like it better than coconut custard."

"Maybe Dave would like some," said Webb's wife, poking her head out of the kitchen.

And then she stared. "Why Dave Neil! What happened? Who gave you that black eye?"

Dave's face reddened. "Oh, I bumped into something in the barn."

"Goodness!" said Hortense. "Would you like a piece of beefsteak to put on it?"

"Certainly not!" cried Webb Walden. "Don't go wasting beefsteak on black eyes. Just give him a piece of apple pie with a big hunk of ice cream on it. That'll fix him up."

"My, we're hardboiled," said Hortense sarcastically. "I should serve you nails for dessert." And with a toss of her head she disappeared into the kitchen.

"Humph," Webb Walden snorted over a cup of coffee. "Nails for dessert. Humph. Women." He winked at Dave and whispered, "Better learn how to handle women, Dave. They're like very sensitive but very powerful engines—the greatest care must be given to their maintenance. And even then," he sighed, "you never know how they're going to perform."

"I guess not," said Dave, smiling at the memory of his mother unscrewing the mop handle so that if it hit Max it would really hurt. "If you ask me, Mr. Walden," said Dave, "women are a lot more complicated than automobile engines."

"You can say that again," said Webb Walden with a cautious glance at the kitchen. "Listen Dave, before I get involved in any arguments or household chores I'm going to get out to the shop. You gobble your dessert and join me as fast as you can get away."

Dave had always enjoyed working on an engine, any automobile engine. But this was much better because it was his pride and joy and because Webb Walden's garage had all kinds of tools within reach. And it was wonderful to work with Webb Walden—he did things so deftly, surely. And he always seemed to give an extra touch to his work or an interesting explanation of it.

The head gasket, Dave knew, was a sheet of asbestos with holes for cylinders. The gasket fitted tightly between the engine head and the valve chambers. Webb Walden worked on it quickly, expertly, and accompanied his work with information:

"Hand me that gasket shellac, will you, Dave?"

"Right."

"When we replace a head gasket in a Duesenberg," said Webb Walden, "we use water pump grease instead of gasket shellac. Reason why is that the Duesy has a heavy head resting on a comparatively small area. But your Model A has a light head resting on a big area. So it needs something stickier than water pump grease. Get it?"

Dave grinned. "I get it," he said. Gosh, he was not only getting the gasket fixed, but he was learning a lesson in mechanics.

"We could have this head planed down for higher compression," Webb went on, "but it would be better to get a regular high-compression head for it."

"Gosh, that would be swell, Mr. Walden," said Dave, "but aren't high-compression heads for Model A's pretty hard to find?"

"They are," said Webb Walden smiling, "but I know where I can find one. It'll cost about thirty bucks but you can work it off here in the shop."

"I'd be glad to," said Dave. A high-compression head—wow! When Mr. Walden got through with the Model A it was going to be a little brother to a Duesenberg.

"Now for that wobble in the wheel," Webb was saying. "The kingpins are probably shot, Dave." Webb smiled. "And if I know my Model A's, those kingpins will be stuck in that axle like impacted wisdom teeth stuck in a jaw bone. We'll have to use the hydraulic

200

press to get 'em out. Once we get the old kingpins out we'll have to use a reamer to cut a nice tight fit for the new ones in the spindle bushings. And those bronze spindle bushings will have to be new, too."

"Hydraulic press." "Reamer." Webb Walden mentioned them so casually that their importance increased in Dave's estimation. They were far beyond the reach of his slim budget. And he thought how lucky he was to be able to use such tools on his own car under the supervision of an expert.

The power of the hydraulic press amazed Dave. The kingpins were deeply embedded in the spindle bushings just as Webb Walden had predicted but the hydraulic press easily forced them out. Dave knew that the kingpins were bearings that took all the wear when the front wheels turned. But he had never actually seen them and he studied the new ones he held ready for Webb Walden, who was cutting a fitting for them in the bronze bushings with the reamer. The kingpins Dave held in his hand were hollow, a few inches long and about one inch in diameter. They were small, those kingpins, but they could cause a lot of trouble; a wobble in a wheel was a worry to any driver and a nagging annoyance to a driver-mechanic like Dave.

"Try the reamer now, Dave." Webb Walden was looking up but carefully holding the reamer, a fragile, expensive tool that looked like an oversize drill.

Dave took over eagerly and under Webb's supervision carefully cut some bronze out of the bushing.

It was fun to use a tool like the reamer. In fact, the whole operation on the Model A—head gasket and kingpins—had been fun, although Dave had been just an assistant-apprentice.

When the work was finished Dave was willing to sit back and steep in satisfaction. But Webb Walden didn't seem to want to rest on his laurels. He was examining the Model A critically. "You've got the makings of a pretty good little racer here, Dave."

The makings? Dave asked himself. Gosh, I think it's good as it stands with the new gasket and kingpins. And it'll be as hot as a firecracker with a high-compression head. Still, Mr. Walden is obviously an expert. What would he suggest as an improvement on a masterpiece?

"Well, let's see." Webb Walden smiled and wiped his greasy hands on a rag. "As I remember it we've talked about two downdraft carburetors, a special manifold, and a high-compression head. Right?"

"Right," said Dave.

"Of course," said Webb, "we could put in a racing cam shaft."

"Of course," mumbled Dave and said to himself, Racing cam shaft. Gosh, what would a racing cam shaft—

"But a magneto would be simpler," Webb Walden was saying.

Simpler than a racing cam shaft? Dave muttered. Well, he supposed it would be—at least it was one word instead of two.

"So we'll replace the electric distributor with a magneto," said Webb Walden.

"How will that help?" Dave asked.

"Well," said Webb Walden smiling, "better spark means better engine performance, doesn't it?"

"Yes," said Dave.

"O.K. The magneto will give you a better spark. For the faster you drive with a magneto, the bigger and better your spark. But the faster you go with an electric distributor the smaller your spark. So we'll replace the distributor with a magneto."

"That'll be swell," said Dave. Then he frowned. "But how am I going to pay for all this, Mr. Walden?"

Webb chuckled, "Same way you'll pay for the high-compression head—work it out in the shop. It won't run into big money—you'll just pay for the parts and I can get 'em for you wholesale."

"But the labor," said Dave. "The work you've done."

"Forget it. That isn't labor, that's fun." Webb chuckled. "Dave, when we get through with this hot rod of yours it'll be really hot; it's just lukewarm now."

"I know," Dave admitted. Suddenly his face lit up. "Gosh, suppose it's hot in time for the hill climb."

"What hill climb?" Webb Walden feigned innocence for a moment then laughed again. "So the news has leaked out."

"You bet it has," said Dave, and added indignantly. "And guess who was one of the first to hear about it— Max Werner. Max is entering that old bathtub of his, the V-8." Dave toned down his indignation. "Gosh, Mr. Walden, with the improvements on my Model A I could run away from Max and his V-8."

Webb Walden had become serious at the mention of Max Werner. Now he said, "Does that twerp think he can enter my hill climb? What makes Max think he can qualify?"

Dave shrugged his shoulders. "Max thinks he can do anything."

"I'm sure he does," said Webb sarcastically. "Incidentally Dave—you don't have to answer this—but was it Max who gave you that black eye?"

"Yes," Dave admitted. His face reddened and the purple of the shiner deepened. Then he smiled thinly. "But you should have seen his nose."

Webb chuckled. "I wish I had." He said seriously, "Listen Dave, don't worry about your Model A against Max's V-8 in the hill climb. With a high-compression head, two Winfield carburetors, and a magneto replacing the distributor—what's the matter?"

Dave's head had dropped on his chest; he was staring at the grease-stained floor; his voice was lifeless. "I won't be in that hill climb, Mr. Walden. I have to go to court tomorrow morning, remember? I'm being tried on three counts: speeding, reckless driving, and illegal use of a cut-out. They'll fine me plenty and they'll also suspend my license for six months."

Webb Walden said slowly, "Oh yes, the trial."

Dave raised his head, forced a smile. "Well, I guess it could be a lot worse. While my license is suspended I'll be working here at the shop. I like it, Mr. Walden— I'm learning a lot. And maybe somebody else could drive the Model A in the hill climb. Maybe there's some boy in Branchville who—"

Bang. Bang. Bang. There was a loud impatient knocking at the nearest door. It rolled up and Hortense stepped in. She stood there, hands on hips, head back. "Webb Walden, do you realize how late it is? It's after six o'clock and we were going to eat an early supper and go to the movies. The baby sitter is already here."

"Oh yes," said Webb, "of course. Be right with you." He turned. "Put the tools away, will you, Dave? I've got to run. See you at three-thirty tomorrow. And good luck in court."

Chapter XVII

STAND up!"

It was a command, terse, tough. It came from the bailiff, a stern symbol in black: black hair, black tie, black suit. The only light touch to the bailiff's color scheme was his silver shield and even that looked grim to Dave as he sat in the courtroom waiting for his case to be called.

He had shuffled in quietly, head down, eyes unseeing, and unobtrusively had slipped into a seat in the first row of wooden benches. In the few minutes that dragged by before the bailiff appeared, Dave had tried to study from the school books he carried with him. But the pages had fluttered like withered oak leaves in a winter wind, the print had blurred, and all that the text of the book seemed to say over and over again was, "Heavy fine, license suspended—heavy fine, license suspended."

In Dave's pocket, touched again and again by sweaty fingers, was the wallet which held one hundred dollars in cash, an enormous amount of money, all but seven dollars of the savings account that had been so slowly and painfully accumulated. It made Dave feel sick to think of that hundred dollars being handed over to the clerk of the court—all those savings given up just because of a reckless, thoughtless violation of the rules of the road.

There was something in the wallet besides his savings. There was the precious document that would be stamped "Suspended"—his driver's license. Six months suspension probably. From the middle of April to the middle of October; the best driving months of the year to a teen-ager and his hot rod. And it would be really hot when Webb Walden got through with it: high-compression head, a magneto, downdraft carburetors. Souped up by an expert, the Model A would run Max Werner's V-8 right off Dead Man's Hill.

Thoughts like these rocked through Dave's mind, sent sickening waves through his stomach, and worked him up to a nervous crisis climaxed by the bailiff's rough command, "Stand up!"

Dave stood up, knees knocking, mouth dry, hands wet. The trial justice strode in. He wore no robes but even without them he was a formidable figure, tall, gaunt, gray, bespectacled. Then Constable Currie appeared. His whiskers were as bushy as ever but somehow they no longer looked comical. The clerk of the court, who sat at the right of the trial justice, was a young man with a sharp nose, big ears, horn-rimmed glasses. To Dave the clerk of the court looked like the devil's assistant preparing a list of the damned as he said in sonorous tones: "The first case, your honor, is the town of Branchville vs.—" Dave's moist fists clenched, his heart stopped beating—"James E. Burke."

Dave's heart started beating again and thumped out a wild rhythm against his ribs as the case of the town of Branchville against James Burke was quickly settled. The accused, an out-of-town driver, had posted a fifty-dollar bond after being arrested by Constable Currie for speeding. The accused had failed to appear; the fifty dollar bond was forfeited.

The wheels of justice turned quickly, coldly, relentlessly. The proceedings gripped Dave with icy fingers —the impassive faces, the cold voices. There was no anger in this bleak courtroom but the very lack of it emphasized the grim, stern way in which justice was administered. One small thankful thought squeezed its way into Dave's misery; he had shown up for his trial; Webb Walden's fifty-dollar bond would not be forfeited.

208

The clerk's deep voice crashed into Dave's thoughts, "The next case is the town of Branchville vs. David Neil."

Dave jumped as if given an electric shock. One of his books slipped and fell to the floor and as he stooped to pick it up the blood rushed sickeningly to his head. Straightening up quickly, he controlled himself with a great effort and, placing the books on the seat he had vacated, moved forward.

"Step this way." The bailiff's voice was not only unfriendly but impatient.

Dave stumbled through a small wooden gate, bumped into a table, then, desperately pulling himself erect in front of the bench, waited for the fall of the sword that had been hanging so long over his head.

It fell. The voice of the trial justice was cold, impersonal. "You are David Neil?" it asked.

"Yes sir," said Dave, cracking his knuckles behind his back.

The trial justice studied a document handed to him by the clerk of the court.

Dave waited, holding his breath.

The trial justice glanced up over the document and the cold voice said, "Mr. Prosecutor, what are the charges against the defendant?"

Mr. Prosecutor? Dave turned tensely and fearfully watched a slight, unimpressive figure in a rumpled blue suit stand up slowly as if every joint ached and, in a tired nasal voice, twang, "Speeding, reckless driving, and illegal use of the cut-out."

Bang-bang-bang. The charges rang out like rifle shots. Dave felt as if he had been shot three times. He thought he would crumple to the floor but he managed to stand, though he weaved a little.

"Speeding, reckless driving, and illegal use of the cut-out." The cold, impersonal voice of the trial justice echoed the charges like the wall of a canyon echoing the sound of a gun. The judicial voice continued, "How do you plead to these charges, David Neil?"

"Guilty," Dave whispered, his chin sinking on his chest.

"Speak up!" the voice commanded.

Dave lifted his chin and managed to say "Guilty" in an audible tone.

"Humph," snorted the prosecutor and flopped down in his chair.

"Hmm," said the trial justice. He removed his glasses, swung them like a pendulum. "As I understand it, you are a member of the Milltown Hot Rod Club."

"Yes sir," said Dave, torturing his fingers as he added in a low voice, "I was, that is."

"Hmm," said the trial justice still swinging his glasses. He spoke over Dave's head to the prosecuting attorney, "Mr. Sefton, as prosecuting attorney for this court would you care to give your opinion of the Milltown Hot Rod Club?"

"I'd be glad to oblige," said the prosecuting attorney, rising painfully and speaking in his tired nasal twang, "In my opinion the Milltown Hot Rod Club is a boil on the community's neck."

Somebody snickered, somebody laughed, several spectators talked and the trial justice tapped the bench with his gavel. As for Dave, he stared nervously at the speaker. The prosecuting attorney didn't look like much but he certainly seemed to know what he was talking about.

"Yes sir," continued the prosecutor, "the Milltown Hot Rod Club has a bad reputation on either side of the town line. The teen-agers who make up its membership represent the three senses: nonsense, insolence, and arrogance."

More snickers, more laughs, and a whack from the gavel.

Dave winced. The prosecuting attorney not only had a picturesque command of the language but an embarrassingly accurate appraisal of the situation.

The trial justice swung his glasses, "That's a pretty caustic analysis of teen-agers, Mr. Prosecutor."

"In my opinion," said the prosecutor, "a certain segment of the teen-age population deserves a caustic analysis, in addition to a good swat on their backsides."

Louder snickers, louder laughs, and a rising buzz of conversation, broken by a smack of the gavel.

"Well then, Mr. Prosecutor," said the trial justice, still swinging his glasses, "judging by the words you have spoken and the way you have spoken them, you would recommend a reformatory term for the defendant?"

Dave quailed. A reformatory?

"No sir," said the prosecuting attorney.

The trial justice swung his glasses and to Dave they suddenly seemed like the scales of justice: left-right, guilty–not guilty, left–right. The cold impersonal voice said, "Then a heavy fine and a driving license suspension of, say, six months?"

Dave shuddered.

"Not exactly," answered the prosecuting attorney.

The glasses stopped swinging; Dave stopped shuddering. And the voice of the trial justice, its cold tone warmed by surprise asked, "Then perhaps, Mr. Prosecutor, you have come into possession of information which mitigates the seriousness of the charges against the defendant."

Now what does that mean? Dave cracked his knuckles.

"Exactly," said the prosecutor. And pulling a rumpled paper from his pocket, he straightened it out, casually adjusted a pair of patched glasses, and read from the paper in his tired, nasal voice, "Report by Constable Currie on defendant David Neil, approved by the prosecuting attorney, town court, Branchville."

Dave took a deep breath—here it comes.

The tired voice continued, "The report reads as

follows: 'I, Constable Currie, have investigated the conditions leading to the arrest of the defendant David Neil. In my opinion, the wrong boy was arrested.' "

Somebody gasped, somebody snorted, somebody snickered, and the comments buzzed about like happy flies on a summer's day. *Bang.* The gavel struck for silence as Dave stared open-mouthed at the prosecuting attorney.

The prosecutor continued, " 'The ringleader of the gang escaped arrest. But he has been warned and steps have been taken to see that he will not escape again. As for the defendant, his conduct since the arrest has shown that his worst weakness was to allow himself to be misled. It is recommended that evidence be given by Mr. Webb Walden.' "

Webb Walden? Dave whispered the name.

The trial justice spoke it to the bailiff, "Is Mr. Webb Walden in court?"

The bailiff shouted the name, "Mr. Webb Walden!"

And as Dave turned apprehensively, the now familiar voice rang out reassuringly from the rear of the courtroom, "Here!"

And there he was, striding confidently down the aisle, tall, straight, neatly dressed, cleanly shaven, the kind of witness any defendant would be glad to have. And was Dave glad to have him!

The voice of the trial justice didn't sound so cold and impersonal now as it said, "Mr. Walden, you have heard the report prepared by the constable and read by the prosecuting attorney?"

"Yes sir," said Webb calmly.

"Do you agree with it?" The glasses swung, left–right.

"Completely," said Webb calmly. "The defendant has worked for me since his arrest and I have had a good chance to size him up."

"And you are satisfied with his attitude as well as his work?"

"Yes sir."

Dave's face was hot and red but he stood straight with his head up and his hands by his side.

"Hmm." The glasses stopped swinging. The cold voice of the trial justice was now warmed up. "Well, I want to say this. Too many teen-agers are being arrested these days. Some of these arrests are for offenses against law and order more serious than speeding and reckless driving. In the big cities not far away there are hold-ups, murders, muggings. But no matter what the offense or crime, it stems from the same source: arrogant rebellion against law and order. And it cannot be condoned. In my opinion it is no excuse for a defendant to say, 'I was misled by the leader of the gang'; that does not alter the fact that the defendant is responsible for his own conduct. Do you understand that, David Neil?"

"Yes sir," said Dave hoarsely.

"I am glad you do," said the trial justice. He smiled thinly. "David, you are a lucky young man. You flagrantly broke the law in a civilized community whose citizens are willing to forgive you and help you. But you broke the law just the same and you are going to pay for it. I hereby fine you five dollars on each count and costs. You will pay the clerk of the court."

"Yes sir," said Dave, reaching for his wallet with sweaty fingers.

"Mr. Walden," said the trial justice.

"Yes sir."

"Do you intend to continue keeping the defendant in your employ?"

"I do."

The trial justice again smiled thinly, "Say, for six months?"

"Yes sir," said Mr. Walden.

"And in that period of time the defendant will be more or less under your supervision?"

"Yes sir."

"Would you be responsible for his driving during that period?"

"Yes sir."

The thin smile broadened. "Good. In that case I shall not suspend David Neil's driving license for a six-month period which I had fully intended to do. Thank you for your cooperation, Mr. Walden. The case is closed."

Chapter XVIII

CASE closed. But not forgotten—not even in the exciting atmosphere of Webb Walden's garage. Dave was no longer an apprentice, his talents restricted to fixing flats and charging batteries. Now he was helping with work that fascinated him as Webb Walden equipped the Model J with domed pistons and over-size valves. But the Model A was not neglected. And Dave's heart and soul went into this work, the installation of the magneto and the high-compression head. For to Dave this was not only a labor of love but work building toward an inspirational goal—victory over Max Werner in the Branchville Hill Climb.

Max had to be beaten. Dave was determined on that point. His arrest and trial had shown Dave many things and foremost among them was this fact: he had been right to challenge Max Werner's leadership of the Milltown Hot Rod Club. But Dave realized now that he had done it for the wrong reasons and in the wrong way. Max was the type of mechanic who blew into a carburetor and got a faceful of gas for his pains. That fact had hit Dave harder at first than Max's show-off contempt for the rules of the road. But Dave's arrest and trial had changed his viewpoint, placed the emphasis on Max's contemptuous attitude toward the law rather than his lack of mechanical ability. That Max was a dumb mechanic had become a minor point. The major point now was that Max was a dangerous type of leader whose rule could easily lead to an accident that would kill or cripple its victim and put its perpetrator behind the bars, not just for a couple of hours but for months—years. Here then was a serious problem and Dave knew that he was the one who had to tackle it; first because he was convinced of its importance and second because he alone of the Hilltown group had built a hot rod capable of the coming challenge.

Work went ahead on the Model J and the Model A, the Duesenberg and the Ford. The Duesenberg was equipped with domed pistons; the Ford, a high-compression head. The Model J got oversize valves, the Model A, a magneto. It was fascinating work to Dave and now it had a definite goal—victory over Max Werner in the Branchville Hill Climb.

Max had to be decisively defeated. And Dave knew that he was the one who had to do it. No one else could, certainly not boys like Billy Forney or Ronnie Felton. They and the other members of the Milltown Hot Rod Club still played follow the leader and the leader was Max. It wasn't right, Dave knew, but it was a fact just the same and something had to be done about it. And the ideal way to do it would be to beat Max so badly in the hill climb that the hot rodders would see their leader for the faker he really was.

Day by day the Model A improved and Dave became so enthusiastic over its progress that he completely forgot another side of the picture. But Webb Walden didn't. "How's your driving, Dave?" he asked one afternoon in May.

"Okay," said Dave, his voice filtering up through an engine. Then he thought, Did I hear correctly? My driving. And sliding out from under the engine on a dolly he looked up at Webb Walden and said, "Are you kidding, Mr. Walden?"

Webb was smiling but he said, "Nope, I'm not kidding. In fact I'm going to give you a driving lesson this very afternoon."

"A driving lesson?" Dave sat up straight on the dolly. "Now I know you're kidding."

"Think so?" said Webb still smiling. "Well, put your

tools away and come along. You'll see whether I'm kidding or not." He turned away, "Angus!"

The Scot did not answer. He was hidden under another car and apparently the only thing he heard was a radio on the work bench broadcasting a game between the Chicago Cubs and the New York Giants.

"Angus!" Webb shouted the name.

"Quiet, mon!" The voice came up through the engine. "Can't ye see I'm listening to the ball game? The Cubs are ahead but the Giants are comin' up fast. They've got two men on, only one oot and the Staten Island Scot is at bat. Listen!"

Webb laughed and listened; so did Dave.

The sound of bat against ball crackled from the radio, immediately followed by the announcer's voice, "A ground ball hit sharply to short. The toss to second for one, the throw to first—double play!"

"Ach," groaned Angus. "Staten Island sank."

" 'Sank' is one word for it," said Webb laughing. He nudged Dave. "Now if it had been Mickey Mantle—"

"Mickey Mantle!" cried Angus, "that upstarrt! What team is he playing for this year, the Minneapolis Millers? Get out of here before I break a wrrench over your head."

"Okay, Angus, we're leaving," laughed Webb. "I'm taking Dave over to the Bennet Farm for a driving lesson."

219

"As long as you dinna take him to the Yankee Stadium it's all right with me," said Angus.

The Bennet farm was a huge place with what Webb called a "private race track," a long dirt road which wound in a circle over hill and dale.

"I've fixed up some old cars for Farmer Bennet," Webb explained as they drove onto the private property in the Model A, "so he lets me test my specials out here." Webb grinned. "I let him know we were coming and the track is closed to pleasure cars, cows, and chickens."

"Good," said Dave. And he smiled at the memory of a wandering chicken that had furnished the Model A with a free frame. Now who was that funny TV actor? Dave didn't have time to remember because Webb was saying, "Stop right here."

Obediently Dave braked to a stop and listened critically to the noise of the idling engine. How sweet it sounded: no spark ping, no piston slap—just the gentle rhythmic click-click-click of the tappets like crickets chirping cheerfully on a warm summer's night.

Dave stepped on the accelerator, not hard, just gently, but enough to feel the new power of the improved engine with its high-compression head, downdraft carburetors. It was all ready. He glanced gratefully at the person who had made all this possible.

Webb Walden's voice was deep and slow. "Okay, Dave, this is it, the first test. I'm the official, you're the novice driver. I want you to drive us around the course once at a moderate speed." Webb smiled. "You can open your cut-out if you like. The cows won't mind and Farmer Bennet is deaf."

Dave smiled a little nervously as he turned the cut-out lever, thinking, Gosh, I haven't done that since the night that Constable Currie—never mind.

"Put your goggles on, Dave." Webb Walden's voice had a gently chiding tone.

"Oh." Dave's face reddened as he reached for the goggles he had forgotten. Once more his mind flashed back to that illegal hill climb when forgotten goggles had almost brought disaster. And again he forced the memory out of his mind and, with fingers that trembled a little, pulled the goggles down over his eyes.

"Ready?" Webb Walden's voice was calm.

Dave nodded. His mouth seemed suddenly dry. His heart began to thump. How "official" was Webb going to be on this test run? Dave glanced at his friend and teacher. Webb was quietly sharing the front seat, an impassive look on his face. It was impossible to tell from that expression what was going on in Webb's mind. So Dave decided to concentrate on driving.

Webb was saying calmly, "My right hand will be the starter's flag. I'll give you a steady 1-2-3 and then drop it. Right?"

Nodding, Dave shifted into first as one last flash of memory showed Max Werner, taunting, boastful, arrogant. What a difference in starters—and in the atmosphere that surrounded the start!

The contrast eased Dave's tension. He smiled to himself. This time he wouldn't peel rubber.

Webb Walden's voice rose over the brash roar of the revved up engine blasting through the unmuffled exhausts. "1-2-3. *Go!*"

Arroomm. The Model A leaped forward, roared up a short rise. *Arroomm.* Dave shifted from first to second and again tromped the accelerator. The car responded with a rush that delighted Dave. But he was disappointed with his shifting—it hadn't been smooth enough or quick enough.

Almost at the top of the rise Dave double-clutched and shifted again into high. For just a couple of seconds the Model A dragged on the slope like a skier shifting from one gait to another. And Dave made a mental note not to shift there the next time around but to go over the top in second.

Down he went now on the other side of the rise with all the old excitement returning from the rush of air, the roar of the improved engine, the feel of the wheel steadied by the new kingpins.

He grinned under his goggles as he heard the Model A back off its pipes. It amused him to think how proud he used to be of a fairly feeble engine with dual exhausts and little else.

At the foot of the hill there was a short straight

stretch before the road wriggled like a snake. Dave faithfully followed the wriggle, drove down another short straight stretch and then skidded into an S bend bordered by a screen of spruces. As the S swung sharply to the right, Dave noticed, straight ahead, a cowpath guarded by a flimsy fence with a sign that said "Beware of the Bull."

Swinging his wheels to the right, Dave came out of the S bend and sent the Model A racing up a short steep hill that curved to the right. Halfway up the hill he shifted smoothly into second and took his Model A to the top with the revved up roar that characterizes a lower gear. As the road leveled off, he shifted to high and drove at a good clip along a short, straight ridge. The ridge road cut through an apple orchard, curved left, and without warning dropped out of sight.

Dave's foot jerked off the accelerator and hit the brake as the Model A hurtled down a hill that resembled a dip in a roller coaster. The hill was not the only hazard. At the bottom of the dip a small green pond waited for any car that could not make a sharp turn to the right.

The old exciting sounds and sensations accompanied Dave down the hill—the rushing of air, the proud noise of the Model A backing off its pipes. But Dave had no time to enjoy these sounds and sensations.

He was stuck on a prong of indecision. How fast should he go down this hill? Should he brake or "shift down" or do both? It would be disastrous to plunge into the pond but neither would it do to take the turn too timidly.

So Dave compromised. He took the dip fairly fast without shifting. The rushing air sang a high sweet song around his ears over the bass accompaniment of the Model A's twin exhausts. Suddenly the sweet song turned sour; he was too near the pond at too high a speed. Alarmed, he applied his brakes; still too fast; he would never make the sharp right turn at the bottom. So he hit the brakes hard as he started the turn and wrenched the Model A's front wheels to the right. The hot rod's rear wheels failed to grip the dirt road and with a sharp whine of protest the tail of the Model A skidded to the left—the brakes had locked; the car was out of control!

With Dave wrestling the wheel like a seasick sailor steering a ship through a storm, the Model A rocked, tossed, spun. As its front wheels faced the hill again, Dave took his foot off the brake and stepped on the gas. The engine roared, the rear wheels clawed at the dirt and back went the hot rod in the direction from which it had come.

But the grade was too steep for the Model A in high gear and before Dave could shift to second the motor gave an embarrassed cough and stalled.

The engine's embarrassment was immediately shared by its operator as the Model A started rolling downhill toward the pond. Again Dave jammed on the brakes. The hot rod obediently jolted to a stop and Dave, his face burning, slumped in the seat staring straight ahead, afraid to glance at his companion.

Webb Walden's calm voice soared through the sudden silence, "One thing that proves, Dave; this car has a nice low center of gravity."

Dave darted a glance to his right. Webb Walden was chuckling. Relieved, Dave pulled on the emergency brake and pushed in the clutch pedal. But before he pushed the starter button he heard Webb say, "Never brake on a curve, Dave. Brake *before you get to the curve.*"

Nodding acknowledgment of this advice, Dave carefully backed downhill. At pond level he straightened out his car and continued on course, his embarrassment ebbing as the Model A once more acted like a racer instead of a stunt car. He drove smoothly over the level stretch beside the pond, shifted into second for another hill, climbed steadily around a gradual curve. At the top of the hill he shifted nicely into high, drove past a chicken house, and rolled down a gentle hill to an intersection near the starting point of the private race course. Here he made a right turn, fanned his brakes, and brought the Model A to a smooth stop. Then he pushed his goggles up on his forehead and waited for the lecture.

None came. Instead Webb Walden smiled and said, "O.K. Dave, I'll take over."

Obediently Dave surrendered the wheel. What was

Webb Walden going to do, take the Model A around the course in a dazzling display of high-speed driving? If so, the first instructional sentence was certainly misleading. For, having turned the cut-out lever so that the exhaust would be muffled and his instructions more audible, Webb Walden smiled and said slowly, "There are old racing drivers, Dave, and there are bold racing drivers; but there is a great shortage of old, bold racing drivers. Understand?"

Dave nodded.

"One more thing before we start, and this you must remember: 'The best driver is the one who wins at the slowest speed.'"

At the slowest speed? Dave puzzled over this remark. "The best driver is the one who wins at the slowest speed?" Could that be possible? It sounded ridiculous. But Webb Walden had certainly said it and Webb was a master mechanic. But perhaps he was not an expert driver. Dave settled back in the seat; he would wait and see.

He saw all right.

Webb Walden pulled a pair of goggles over his eyes, revved up the engine, shifted into first. Simple things— but there was something about the way Webb did them that indicated great skill and long experience.

Webb smiled, "O.K. Dave—start me off."

Dave raised his right hand, "Ready?"

Webb nodded.

"1-2-3. *Go!*"

Arroomm. They went—swiftly but smoothly, without breaking traction. And when Webb shifted from first to second it was also smooth and swift. And accompanied by a calm, clear comment, "When you shift up, Dave, don't bother to double-clutch; it doesn't help, and it wastes seconds. Double-clutch only when you shift down."

Dave nodded while the Model A soared up the first rise in second and Webb continued the lesson: "Stay in second on a hill like this until—"

They had reached the top and, with a grin, Webb quickly shifted into high, finishing his instructional sentence with a neat illustration.

Down the hill they rolled, into the wriggle of the road. Here Webb slowed down and said, "You followed this curve too faithfully, Dave. Remember that a straight line is the shortest distance between two points, as long as you *know* there's nothing coming toward you. Watch."

As Dave watched, Webb speeded up and skillfully steered the car through the road's wriggle in almost a straight line by slanting from left to right then from right to left.

As they emerged from the wriggle of the road Webb slowed down and said, "What we were working on there, Dave, is something called centrifugal force. Ever tie a string around a stone and swing it around your head? If the stone breaks loose it flies straight out. That is centrifugal force. Your car gets going straight and wants to keep going that way. And in certain bends like this one you can help by steering as I just did. You not only save distance but you increase tire traction and keep the car as undisturbed as possible."

Dave nodded and filed the facts away: straight line, centrifugal force, increased tire traction, car undisturbed as possible. Undisturbed? Dave winced as he thought of all the disturbance he had caused with his spin near the pond.

Shifting smoothly, Webb Walden was accelerating along the short straight stretch before the curve. Too fast, too close to the curve? Suddenly Webb's right foot came off the accelerator and hit the brake. Simultaneously Webb shifted down, smoothly, swiftly. He kicked the clutch, flipped the gear shift to neutral, gunned the engine; he let the clutch out and in again, and shifted to second. The Model A slowed up, veered to the middle of the road, and growled impatiently into the apex of the S curve's first loop. Suddenly *arroom*. Webb Walden stepped on the gas and sent the car roaring out of the curve. Then he slowed down and explained his strategy.

"What I did there, Dave," said Webb, "was to pick a cut-out point on that straight stretch of road."

"What's a cut-out point?" Dave asked.

"A cut-out point," said Webb Walden, "is a place where you take your foot off the accelerator and step on the brake." Webb smiled. "Remember what happened when you braked in that curve down by the pond?"

Dave nodded, his face reddening.

"Well, spins like that don't happen if you pick your cut-out point properly and brake before you go into the corner.

"Is it an actual point?" Dave asked.

"Yes," Webb answered. "You decide where you should cut out the engine and then fix that point in your field of vision with some stationary guide like a tree, post, or barn."

The Model A speeded up again and as it entered the second loop of the S bend Webb Walden said, "Another way to get around a curve is to use a 'Grand Prix drift' or 'power slide.'"

The phrases fascinated Dave. "Grand Prix drift," "power slide." Dave wanted them explained right away.

Webb grinned, slowed down, and said, "I knew that would be your reaction. Every time I've ever mentioned a Grand Prix drift or power slide to a youngster he immediately wants to jump from primary training to advanced."

"Would that be advanced training?" Dave asked, curbing his eagerness.

"Of course," said Webb. "A power slide or Grand Prix drift takes plenty of practice."

"Could you demonstrate it for me, Mr. Walden?"

Webb smiled. "Not on this course, Dave; it's too short and sharp."

"Well then, could you just tell me how it's done?"

Webb grinned, braked, stopped the car and said, "Okay. I guess I shouldn't have brought it up. But now that I have, I'll explain. In a Grand Prix drift you steer with your throttle."

"Steer with your throttle?" Dave was incredulous.

"Right. It's like driving on ice. You go into a shallow bend at high speed and deliberately put your car in a skid."

"Deliberately?"

"Deliberately," Webb chuckled. "That's why the Grand Prix drift is only for highly skilled drivers. You know how embarrassing an accidental skid can be."

"Yes," said Dave. He could feel his face reddening.

"Well, this is a deliberate skid when you're going as fast as a hundred miles an hour."

"Wow!" Dave exclaimed.

"Exactly," said Webb smiling. "You go into the shallow bend at high speed. Then you set your drift by twisting the wheel a little too sharply in the direction the bend is taking."

"Set your drift?" said Dave in awed tones.

"Right. Once you start that skid or drift, you return

230

the wheel to its previous position and hold it there. In other words, your drift is set and from then on you steer with your throttle."

"How come?" asked Dave eagerly.

"Because you're in a skid, Dave. You're breaking traction. If you give it more throttle, your skid increases and the angle of your turn become sharper. Less throttle, less skid, a more gradual turn. In other words you steer with your throttle."

"I see," said Dave slowly. He was in an awed, happy daze embellished by fascinating phrases. "Power slide," "Grand Prix drift," "shallow bend," "set your drift," "steer with your throttle." How much more impressive those expressions were than the ones Max Werner used to mouth: "peel rubber," "wind it out." Max Werner. Gee, that guy would probably think a Grand Prix drift was a French boat that had cut loose from its moorings.

The Model A was now moving slowly through the S bend and Webb was saying, "But I really shouldn't have brought that up, Dave. That's advanced training and we're in primary. We're going to practice the slower kind of cornering, picking the proper cut-out point, driving with the wheel instead of the throttle. We'll brake at our cut-out points, shift down, drive carefully into the apex of the corner. Then we'll pour on the power, apply throttle until we run out of revs, then shift to high."

231

Dave listened, nodded, and added the nice new phrase to his fast-growing sports car vocabulary, "run out of revs." In just a few second he acquired another expression, for as Webb drove the Model A out of the S bend he pointed at the cowpath marked by the sign saying "Beware of the Bull," and said, "That would make a good escape road, Dave, if it weren't for the bull."

"Escape road." This term's meaning was obvious; if you couldn't make the turn you took the escape road.

Now they climbed the curving hill, passed the apple orchard, and approached the roller-coaster dip toward the pond. Freed from the responsibility of driving Dave noticed the beauty of the scene, the green grass on the side of the hill, a cow peacefully chewing its cud, the placid pond. But it was deceptive beauty, Dave knew, to the driver of a racing car. A minor mistake would skid the Model A off the road and plunge it into the pond.

How would Webb Walden meet these hazards? Dave took a deep breath, got a good grip on the cowl, and watched closely.

It was worth watching. For Webb Walden was shifting down and the difficult operation was done deftly, smoothly, with no jerks or grinding of the gears. What's more, Webb explained it as he did it. "Here's where you double-clutch, Dave, in shifting down. Watch."

Webb pushed in the clutch pedal, shifted to neutral.

Then he gunned the engine, double-clutched, and shifted smoothly down to second. With its transmission turned into a brake, the Model A, which had started to plunge recklessly down the hill in high, slowed to a reasonable speed in second. And Webb Walden said calmly, "When you double-clutch you gun the engine to get the gears going at a matching speed so they won't grind on meshing. For example, if your engine is turning a thousand rpm's in high, it will need, say, two thousand rpm's for the same speed in second. So you shift to neutral and gun the engine to speed up the gears you're going to use."

With the Model A using its transmission as a brake, the sharp curve at the base of the hill was approached carefully. Driving on the left-hand side of the road, positioning for the curve, Webb smiled and said, "Don't forget, Dave; there are old racing drivers and bold racing drivers but there is a great shortage of old, bold racing drivers."

Dave nodded and relaxed his grip on the cowl. The lesson was clear. If you hurtled recklessly into a sharp curve, the laws of physics caught up with you and sent you into a dangerous humiliating spin. But if you approached the corner carefully, took it slowly—

"Hold on!" The warning was barked just before the engine roared. *Arrooom.* The Model A leaped forward. Cutting across to the right Webb Walden had reached the apex of the corner and poured on the power. His mouth open, Dave clutched the cowl as the hot rod raced away from the pond and clawed up the final hill. The sudden speed had Dave hanging on for all he was worth but at the same time his mind was busy analyzing Webb Walden's cornering, the smooth shifting, the careful positioning and then *arroomm*—pour on the power! It all added up to one short succinct phrase—Safety Fast. And Dave was eager to get behind the wheel and try to put Webb Walden's theories into practice on this private race course.

But someone was ahead of him, not behind the wheel of the Model A but at the wheel of a long, beautiful, scarlet sports car. Its driver was a picture of sartorial splendor: a shiny white crash helmet matched an immaculate white coverall; a dark blue silk scarf with a white monogram jauntily protected the driver's neck; and most impressive of all was the miniature windshield that hung down from the crash helmet over the driver's face.

"What is it?" Dave asked. He wasn't sure to what he was referring, the gorgeous car or the magnificent figure in it. In any case he was staring wide-eyed at the dazzling spectacle.

Webb Walden was smiling as he brought the Model A to a stop. The hot rod suddenly looked like a small, ragged mongrel confronted by a sleek, handsome, and disdainful great Dane.

"It's a British sports car called a Jaguar," said Webb

234

Walden, "and the driver is Negley Foxcroft, the TV actor."

Negley Foxcroft? said Dave to himself. That was the name I was trying to remember. Negley Foxcroft, the TV actor. Gosh, he sure looked sharp in that racing driver costume. But what the heck was that windshield doing over his face?

Webb Walden explained in a low voice, "That's an English contraption known as a "talc visor." We call it an Oscar boom. Don't ask me why. Anyway, it works just as well as goggles and is twice as impressive." Webb chuckled. "Negley Foxcroft probably puts a windshield wiper on it when it's raining." Webb turned his chuckle into a shout, "Hi, Negley, out for a practice run?"

Negley Foxcroft's volatile voice filtered through the Oscar boom, sounding as if it had been affected by the visor's origin, "I thought I'd take my Jag on a bit of a practice run, Webb. Mind if I go on ahead of you, old boy?"

"Not at all," grinned Webb Walden, "If I must eat dust I prefer the superior kind generated by a Jaguar."

"Ho-ho-ho." A fruity laugh rumbled out under the talc visor. "Rather witty today, aren't we? Well—" Negley Foxcroft touched his white crash helmet in a gallant salute—"cheerio, Webb."

The Jaguar's engine revved up smoothly, powerfully. Impressed, Dave said, "Gosh, I'll bet Mr. Fox-croft will go around the course in nothing flat."

"We'll see," said Webb Walden still smiling.

Arrooom. The Jaguar took off, its rear tires screech-ing like parakeets. A cloud of dust rose and settled on the humble inhabitants of the Model A. Dave coughed and in an awed tone said, "Gosh, he peeled rubber, uh—" he coughed again—"I mean he broke traction."

"That's not the only thing he'll break," said Webb Walden dryly. "Take over, Dave. We'll wait for the dust to settle and follow at a discreet distance. Pick your cut-out points, brake before the curve, accelerate at its apex, and don't try any power slides, please. Save those for Watkins Glen."

Dave did as directed. He got the Model A off the mark quickly but smoothly without breaking traction. He went over the first rise in second gear without losing time and power in shifting. Not until he reached the top did he shift to high, without double-clutching. In the short straight stretch he picked a tall pine tree as a cut-out point, braked near it, slowed down to a speed he could handle in the wriggle of the road. He found that braking at the cut-out point permitted him to position properly for the wriggle, which he nego-tiated as instructed, remembering what Webb Walden had said about a straight line being the shortest distance between two points. As he rolled smoothly through the wriggle, he could still see the Jaguar's proud plume of dust, hear its arrogant roar as it ripped through the S curve.

Before going into the S bend Dave picked another cut-out point, braked at it, slowed, positioned, and accelerated at the curve's apex. He was surprised at the smooth yet swift pace with which this system carried him around curves. He was so fascinated by the way it worked that he failed to notice that the dust raised by the Jaguar had vanished, the arrogant roar subsided.

But as the Model A passed the cowpath escape road Webb Walden tapped Dave on the arm, signaled him to a stop and asked, "Where is our gallant knight and his Jaguar? Take a look at that fence on your left, Dave. Somebody just went through it."

Negley Foxcroft? Who else? Over the noise of the Model A's idling engine now came the frantic honking of a horn from an invisible part of the cowpath.

"We'd better go see what's wrong," said Webb Walden, and he quickly got out and trotted up the escape road parallel with a sturdy stone wall. Following, Dave came upon the strangest sight he had ever seen.

The scarlet Jaguar was blatting around a green pasture angrily pursued by a big black bull. Frantically winding his wheel and honking his horn was Negley Foxcroft. His white crash helmet and talc visor were still in place but his knotted blue silk scarf had come undone and was fluttering brightly in the breeze.

Dave stared stupefied at the fantastic spectacle. But beside him Webb Walden laughed and said, "It's the third battle of Bull Run. Look out, Dave!"

The Jaguar was escaping by superior speed, and the frustrated bull was turning on the two pedestrians.

"Over the wall!" cried Webb Walden.

As they scrambled over the stone wall, the bull bellowed and charged, its sharp horns lowered menacingly. But it encountered the wall and skidded to a stop, snorting and pawing.

Safe on the other side of the wall Webb Walden was laughing again. "We lured him away, Dave. Nice 'cape work' as they say in Spain."

"Look out!" This time Dave gave the warning. The bull had galloped a few yards along the wall until it found an opening where two cross bars had been lowered. Stumbling over the lowered bars the bull attacked from the flank.

Back they scrambled over the wall. "We can't go on doing this forever," said Webb Walden, slightly out of breath. "Dave, you wave your arms and pull that bull in the opposite direction while I sneak along the wall and put those bars back up."

With Dave acting as decoy, Webb Walden ducked unobtrusively along the wall and barred the bull from further pursuit. Then, laughing over their experience, they made their way back to the race course.

Negley Foxcroft was waiting for them in his scarlet Jaguar. It had a dent in its front from the frail fence it had broken through and one gash in a fender where it had been gored by the bull, but Negley Foxcroft was unharmed. He had retied his silk scarf, recovered his poise, even his British accent. "Bit of a bull fight, what?" he said from under his talc visor. "Might use that skit in one of my TV shows. Would fit nicely. I'm doing a series sponsored by Princess Pancakes on big game hunting in Africa. Perhaps you've seen it. I'm taking the part of Reginald Playfair, a playboy from Oxford who finds himself in the jungle. Have you caught the show, Webb?"

Webb grinned. "Sorry to say I haven't, Negley." Webb climbed into the Model A. "Are you going on or have you had enough for today?"

"Oh, good heavens no!" cried Negley Foxcroft. "A bit of a bullfight can't discourage me. The show must go on and all that sort of rot."

Arrooom. The Jaguar roared again like a jungle beast in a TV script. "Carry on!" cried Negley Foxcroft. Once more the hand touched the crash helmet in a jaunty salute and with a scream of protest from its tires the Jaguar departed in a cloud of dust.

"Gosh," said Dave with a cough, "he peeled—uh, broke traction again."

Webb Walden wagged his head. "He'll never learn. Good old Negley. Last time I saw him he had a French accent—he was playing the Count of Monte Cristo. Next month he may be an Italian opera singer—it'll be tough yodeling under that talc visor." Webb laughed. "Let's go, Dave, the dust has settled."

As Dave drove the Model A up the hill he wondered how Negley Foxcroft would take the steep dip and the sharp curve down by the pond. Dave knew how he was going to take it this time—cautiously. He was going to shift down into second, pick a cut-out point, brake at it, and get to the curve's apex before accelerating. But how would Negley Foxcroft take the roller-coaster dip?

Negley Foxcroft took it conservatively. He shifted down, and, though the abused transmission growled in protest, it slowed Negley's speed as he carefully passed the cow still peacefully chewing its cud. Then the TV actor cautiously maneuvered into the curve before accelerating.

Not bad, said Dave to himself as he emulated the Jaguar's example. A lot better than I did on the last time around. Perhaps Negley Foxcroft isn't so wacky a driver after all.

Accelerating out of "pond corner," Dave followed the Jaguar to the finish line and at Webb Walden's instruction pulled alongside the British sports car. "Going around again Negley?" Webb asked.

"Oh good heavens yes," said Negley under his talc visor. "I'm going to step up the pace on this run and time myself with my chronograph." Negley Foxcroft flicked a wrist out from his white coverall, exposing an impressive timepiece which he proceeded to set for the test ahead.

"Chronograph," said Dave. "Where have I heard that word before?"

"It's the same gadget Cavendish tried to chisel from the Model J," Webb explained, "but this goes on the wrist instead of the dashboard. It's a stop watch with everything but chimes. Much fancier than this kind." Webb pulled an ordinary stop watch out of his pocket and in a casual voice said to Negley Foxcroft, "We're going to time ourselves over the run too, Negley. Why don't we make a little contest out of it?"

"Oh, my dear chap," said Negley Foxcroft, giving the Model A a disdainful look, "surely you're not serious? How much of a handicap would you want?"

"None," said Webb Walden calmly.

"None!" cried Negley Foxcroft with another glance at the humble Model A. He snorted. "Very well, as you wish." Once again the white crash helmet was touched in debonair salute as Negley said, "Let us synchronize our watches. Five fifteen and forty-five seconds. Fifty. Fifty-five—"

"*Go!*" cried Webb Walden.

Arrrooomm. The Jaguar broke traction as usual and

roared away up the first hill, once again waving its proud plume of dust.

Dave let out an overawed breath. "Gosh, am I going to compete against that?"

"Sure," said Webb Walden blithely. "Just drive the way you did on the last run, braking at the cut-out points, positioning properly, accelerating from the apex of the curve. And remember, Dave, the best driver is the one who wins at the slowest speed."

Dave shook his head in disbelief, saying to himself, Look at that Jaguar go. Or rather, try and look at it. It was gone over the hill, leaving only a contemptuous cloud of dust to drift back and settle on its humble competitor.

But Webb Walden seemed unconcerned. His stop watch in his left hand, he raised his right, "Ready?"

Dave revved up the engine, shifted into first, then nodded his head.

"1-2-3. *Go!*"

Arroom. The Model A leaped forward. Up the hill it roared and down again through the wriggle and along the straight stretch to the S turn. Using all of the lessons he had learned, Dave made this the fastest run for the Model A. But he couldn't gain on the Jaguar. The drone of its powerful engine was distant, the dust it raised had settled by the time the Model A arrived at the S bend. There was no sign of the scarlet sports car until Dave reached the top of the roller-coaster dip that descended so precipitously to the placid pond. There at the top of the hill Dave finally caught sight of the Jaguar and its actions made Dave brake and stare.

For the Jaguar was in serious trouble at the foot of the hill. The Jaguar was in a spin. It was skidding, whirling, whining—splashing, steaming; it was in the pond!

Glub. Bubbles were coming up from under the talc visor. Glub-blub. The talc visor floated away to disclose a familiar face with a surprisingly different voice. The British accent had apparently drowned; for, as Negley Foxcroft staggered up from the pond, he was gasping and cursing like a sailor unexpectedly hurled from a snug ship into a cold cruel sea. "Gol blame blankety blank! Help me out of this blasted muck! Why the blankety blank didn't that ignorant farmer have this blankety blank pond drained?"

Negley Foxcroft stood dripping on the grassy bank, his once white coverall streaked, splotched, soaked, his blue silk scarf a limp rag hanging from his neck. Behind him in the pond floated his white crash helmet. Shining on the surface, like a submarine about to submerge, floated the talc visor.

Negley Foxcroft stumbled out to the road and his shoes went squish-squeak, squish-squeak like a pump with a leaking valve. He spoke and water sprayed forth like a badly adjusted bathtub shower. "That blankety blank cow!" he sputtered.

The cow? What did the poor old cow have to do with the calamity, Webb Walden wanted to know.

"What did that blankety blank cow have to do with it?" Negley Foxcroft exploded like a geyser in Yellowstone Park, "that blankety blank cow was my cut-out point—and the blasted beast moved!"

Pastoral peace had finally been restored. Loud laughs had turned into chuckles. A coughing tractor had pulled the scarlet intruder from the shallow pond. A barking collie had herded the bull back to its barn. Now Dave and Webb Walden were on the way back to the garage in the Model A and Webb smiled and said, "You didn't believe what I said at first, did you Dave?"

"About what Mr. Walden?" Dave was still smiling at the mental image of Negley Foxcroft wading back into the pond to retrieve his precious talc visor.

"About the best driver being the one who wins at the slowest pace."

"Oh," said Dave. "No." He shook his head. "I guess I didn't."

"But you see my point now," Webb chuckled, "and I don't mean a cow for a cut-out point."

Dave laughed. "I see it."

"Good. Remember that a Model A rounding a sharp

corner at twenty-five miles an hour can always beat even a Jaguar plunging into a pond. Remember that, Dave, when you make your qualifying run in the Branchville hill climb. Max Werner will be there showing off with his V-8, breaking traction, skidding around corners, playing to the grandstand. Don't let Max needle you into the same kind of driving. Take it easy. Select your cut-out points, brake at them, accelerate at the apex of the curve. And always remember that the best driver is the one who wins at the slowest speed."

Chapter XIX

MAX WERNER. The mental image the name presented still disturbed Dave. And he resented the disturbance. Max Werner was a swaggering braggart, a loud-mouthed show-off who wore a silly peaked cap over ridiculous sideburns. But he was still the leader of the Milltown Hot Rod Club; there was no getting away from that fact. Boys like Billy Forney and Ronnie Felton hadn't changed their opinion of Max Werner. Only Dave Neil had, making him a minority of one.

Dave knew that if he were beaten by Max Werner in the Branchville hill climb a great opportunity would be wasted. For there was only one real reason why fellows like Ronnie Felton and Billy Forney were still under the influence of Max Werner; and the reason was this—Max hadn't been shown up.

As for that gook wagon of Max Werner's, it had a new paint job, purple with gilt trim; it looked pretty sharp. But what was under the hood? Was it like its owner, flashy in the promise, poor in the performance? Had the engine been efficiently repaired? Had it been improved? Dave didn't know the answer to any of these questions. All he knew was that Max seemed very proud of his V-8 as he skidded it into Chet Coley's crowded filling station where Dave was waiting to have his Model A inspected for the hill climb.

Jamming on his brakes to make his tires scream, Max gunned his engine, tipped back his peaked cap, and said to Webb Walden, "Cars bein' inspected here for the hill climb?"

Dave watched and listened. How would Webb Walden handle this situation?

Calmly and coolly. "Right," said Webb and added sarcastically, "Your brakes seem to be working well, Max."

"Best brakes in the county," Max boasted, lighting a cigarette.

"Put that cigarette out, Max," said Webb without raising his voice.

"Why?" said Max arrogantly.

"You should be able to figure that out for yourself," said Webb coldly. "There's high octane gas all around you."

Nyaaa, said Max under his breath. He took one last defiant drag from the cigarette and sullenly ground

247

it out. "Okay, bring on all the Sunday blue laws, all the panty-waist rules. I want my heap inspected."

"You're next after the Model A," said Webb calmly.

"I thought so!" cried Max. "Favoritism right off the bat. I'll bet the hill climb is rigged. You guys are in cahoots."

"Sure," grinned Webb, "we're going to let the air out of your tires when your back is turned. And Dave here has a whole bag of tacks he's going to scatter across the road before you make your qualifying run."

"Qualifying run!" cried Max. "You're askin' a driver like me to make a qualifying run? How much nerve can ya get? What'sa matter, you guys afraid I'm gonna run ya down?"

Webb's voice stayed calm. "We're not just protecting ourselves, Max. Strange as it may seem—to me as well as you—we're protecting you too."

"Oh sure," scoffed Max. "Listen, I can take care of myself."

"Perhaps," said Webb, "but we're not leaving that to chance. And I might as well tell you right now that you can't drive in this hill climb without safety equipment."

"Safety equipment?" sneered Max. "What is this, a hill climb or a May-pole dance?"

Listening, Dave stared. Would Webb Walden get annoyed? No, he was chuckling as he said in his un-ruffled voice, "Listen Max, I'll inspect your car today without safeguards but if you show up tomorrow without them I'll have to disqualify you."

"Of course you'll disqualify me," squawked Max. "I can see that comin' a mile off. In fact, that's what I told all the fellas at the hot rod club; I'll be disqualified before I even get a chance to compete."

"Now listen, Max." Webb's tone toughened as he leaned over the violent violet bathtub. "I've let you shoot your mouth off since you skidded in your show-off way into this station. And you've said some pretty stupid things. But there's one thing you're going to stop saying—you're going to stop yakking about favoritism. You'll be treated just like any other competitor."

"Yeah?" said Max truculently. "How?"

"First, your car will be inspected for mechanical defects. We'll check your brakes for tightness, your steering for looseness, and your wheels for balance."

"Nothin' there to worry me," Max boasted. "This rod is in A-1 shape."

"We'll see," said Webb, a light smile flickering at the corner of his mouth. "Then we'll check your car for safety equipment."

"What kinda safety equipment?" sneered Max.

"Crash helmet, safety belt, first-aid kit, and fire extinguisher."

"Fire extinguisher!" cried Max. "Wha'do I look like, a fireman?"

"Don't ask me what you look like," said Webb coolly; "you might get an answer you wouldn't like."

"Oh yeah?"

"Yeah."

"Humph." Max grunted but changed the subject from the personal to the impersonal. "Listen, where am I gonna find all that junk?"

"That's your problem," said Webb, "and don't try and tell me it's a last-minute one. That mandatory safety equipment was all listed on your application blank—you just didn't read it."

Nyaa, said Max under his breath. And aloud he asked belligerently, "Listen, how long is this joint gonna be open for inspection?"

"About another two hours," said Webb. "Why?"

"Well," said Max, "I gotta wait anyway. Davey boy here and his heap are ahead of me." Max contemptuously jerked his thumb at Dave and the Model A. "So in the meantime I could pick up that silly safety stuff. Hey, I wonder—"

"Hay is for horses," said Webb quietly.

"Yeah?" Max ignored the reproof. "But say, would a football helmet be O.K. instead of the regulation crash helmet?"

"I guess we could accept that." Webb chuckled. "Of course it would be showing you favoritism."

"Oh yeah?" said Max. He switched on his ignition. "Well, so long. I'll be back inside of an hour." He winked. "Make sure that Davey boy has his brakes in good shape—he uses 'em a lot, y'know."

"On your way, Max," said Webb, his tone toughening again. "And while you're installing your safety equipment try fitting a new attitude into that two-cylinder brain of yours. It'll make your life much easier."

Max's answer to this advice was to rev up the V-8's engine, shift into first, snap out the clutch, and peel rubber. With a roar from its engine and a scream from its rear tires the bathtub departed.

Webb walked over to the Model A, smiled sadly, shook his head, and said, "The poor sap. If ever a guy had the wrong slant Max is it."

"He sure has a chip on his shoulder," Dave agreed.

Webb frowned. "I wonder what's behind that belligerent, wise-guy attitude?"

"Don't ask me," Dave shrugged his shoulders. He had the hood up on his Model A and was checking the spark plugs. "I guess Max was just born that way."

"I doubt that," said Webb. "You're not born that way—you get that way. Y' know, Dave—" Webb leaned on the Model A—"before I got married I was interested in only one thing, that thing you're working on—the automobile engine."

Dave looked up from the spark plugs.

Webb went on, smiling a little. "But having a wife like mine and talking things over with her—that's what we call our arguments—" Webb chuckled—"sort of changes your views on life. Of course, having kids makes a difference too. Your interests in engines holds up, Dave, but you also get interested in something much more important than engines—human beings. And believe me, Dave, male or female, they're much more complicated than an automobile." Webb gave Dave a friendly tap on the arm. "Well, let's get the inspection over with—O.K?"

"O.K.," said Dave straightening up. He wasn't worried about the Model A's passing inspection. But he was concerned about Webb's comments on Max Werner. Webb didn't agree that Max was born a foul ball—he grew that way, got that way somehow. In other words, human beings often behaved like auto engines—balked or purred; but the analogy could be misleading. A clogged carburetor could easily be cleaned by a good mechanic, but straightening out kinks in a human being was quite a different matter; and one that required cooperation on the part of the patient. Max had become a foul ball; how long he remained one would depend a great deal on himself and his reactions to the things that were bound to happen to him.

Chapter XX

LADIES and gentlemen," said the voice over the public address system. Dave recognized the rich theatrical accent of Negley Foxcroft. He of the talc visor and the scarlet Jaguar had naturally become the official announcer for the event about to take place, and his volatile voice had adapted its accent to the occasion— it was deep, full, portentous. "You are about to witness the first hill climb ever staged in Fairfield County. The competitors will drive their cars from the stone bridge at the foot of the hill, up through the S bend to a point on the ridge one measured mile from the starting line.

"There will be two classes of competitors: novices and veterans. In each class the driver of the car with the best time for the mile will be declared the winner. But remember, ladies and gentlemen, each driver may make two runs up the hill, the first this morning, the second this afternoon. The faster time of these two runs will be the time considered in determining the winner.

"The course is now closed to pleasure traffic. Spectators along the course are respectfully reminded that they are not allowed to cross the course during the hill climb. Whichever side of the road you find yourself on now, please stay on it. Spectators are also warned to stay away from the outside corners of the curves.

"Please cooperate with the authorities who have given us permission to put on this event. Let us remember the motto 'Safety Fast,' and keep this hill climb fast but safe so that in the future we can put on bigger and better sports car events.

"Incidentally, ladies and gentlemen, this hill climb is being sponsored by the local Parent-Teachers Association. The money you pay for your souvenir program will go toward the purchase of new playground equipment.

"Now as you all know—"

Dave didn't hear the rest of Negley Foxcroft's long-winded announcement. For a small but sharp voice had invaded the cockpit of the Model A where Dave sat waiting for the starter's flag, "Kin I have your autograph?"

"My autograph?" Dave jerked back his crash helmet in surprise and stared at the freckle-faced boy with the carrot colored hair who was thrusting a program and a pencil toward the steering wheel. Carrot Top wasn't kidding either; he meant it. So Dave said "Sure" and with a grin signed his name to the extended program. He was glad to see that his hands were steady although moist from the mounting tension. And he said to himself, An autograph—imagine my being asked for an autograph in the town of Branchville. Why, just a couple of months ago this same town threw me in jail.

"How fast kin it go?" asked Carrot Top, withdrawing his now precious program.

"Well," Dave grinned, "I haven't had it—"

"Has it got a supercharger?" asked Carrot Top without waiting for an answer to the first question.

Dave smiled. "Not yet."

"Has it really got two carburetors?"

Dave nodded, "It really has."

"How much did it cost yuh?" Carrot Top wanted to know.

Dave chuckled. "Well," he began, "it's sort of a long story."

"So long," said Carrot Top suddenly. He was evidently not fond of long stories. "I got to go get an autograph from the guy who drives the Jag."

"The Jag." Dave shook his head in wonder. How quickly kids caught on—already calling the Jaguar a "Jag." And that kid had actually come up for an auto-

255

graph. It was hard to believe. It was hard to believe, too, that the hill climb was actually being staged. But it was real all right. Negley Foxcroft's rich voice was not only speaking to a big crowd near the stone bridge but by means of other loudspeakers spotted along the course was addressing hundreds of spectators waiting at the S bend and along the ridge road at the top of the hill. It was a surprisingly big crowd and a varied one, old and young, rich and poor, farmers and commuters to the city, athletes and aesthetes. Dave had recognized Milltown High baseball players and female classmates who contributed poetry to the high school paper. They were all there, strolling around the pits, inspecting the cars, calling out cordially, "Hi Dave, good luck."

And Dave, glowing at the greeting, thought, Why half of those people hardly spoke to me a month ago. And here they are calling me by my first name and wishing me good luck. What a change!

There was another change just as startling. It was in the reception given Dave's competitor in the novice class, Max Werner, the only other survivor besides Dave, of four novice entries. The other two, Billy Forney and Ronnie Felton, had been disqualified, one for mechanical reasons and the other for driving ability —or lack of it. But Max Werner had passed both tests and in the end had been surprisingly cooperative about taking them. Why? Did Max Werner have something up his sleeve? Or was there hidden beneath all that swagger and bluster a streak of envy for what Dave had accomplished? Max had been a wise guy when he first showed up for the car inspection. But it was evident that he had been impressed in spite of himself. The fairness of the hill climb officials, led by Webb Walden, must have had some effect even on a foul ball like Max, Dave reasoned. And Dave knew that the organizing of the hill climb made an impression because organizing was Max Werner's specialty. And the organization of the hill climb was a hundred times more ambitious and efficient than anything that had ever been arranged by Max Werner. Dave could see that Max was impressed by the size of the crowd and the communications setup: in addition to the public address system there were three signal stations along the course, each manned by two officials in white coveralls. One of these men received and sent messages over a telephone wire, the other stood ready to signal the drivers with flags, yellow to slow down, red to stop. The organization was remarkable and Max was obviously awed by it.

Max was sitting in his gook wagon. It now had a big white No. 5 on it but it looked more like a movie star's bathtub than a racing car. And Max, sitting behind the wheel wearing a red and gold football helmet, looked like a film comedian. That was the odd part about it, Dave told himself. In Dave's eyes Max had become more comical than villainous and it was possible that Max himself was slowly becoming aware of that fact. Because the crowd from Milltown High, the athletes and aesthetes, were ribbing the driver of No. 5: "Hey Max, where'd yuh steal the bathtub? Why don'tcha fill it with water and take a bubble bath?"

"Hey Max, what's that on your head? Football season's over. This isn't a gridiron, it's a hill climb."

And so forth. Max's reaction to these jibes was varied according to the size and athletic ability of the tormentor. Max reddened and smiled sheepishly at some, scowled at others, threatened still others with a good stiff punch in the snoot.

Dave watched, wondering. It was the first time he had ever seen Max in such an ignominious position. And Dave wondered why he didn't enjoy the ex-villain's humiliation. Probably because Max was no longer a villain but just a sap. And there was no fun in showing up a sap. Besides he wasn't quite shown up yet.

Webb Walden was suddenly standing by the Model A, leaning into the hot rod's cockpit. He was smiling and his calm voice minimized the effect of the news he brought. "We just got a message from signal station 2. The members of the Milltown Hot Rod Club are perched on the stone shelf over the second bend."

"Oh?" said Dave. An uneasy feeling deepened the pre-competition tension.

"Yup." Webb grinned. "Your old pals are sitting up there behind a big oilcloth banner advertising their organization. And they're acting like cheap copies of their president—smoking, yelling, drinking beer from cans. They've already had to be warned for tossing empty beer cans down on the course."

"They would," said Dave in disgust.

"Exactly," said Webb, smiling thinly. "Max is still their leader and they're going to act like him until they see him for the sap he really is."

Dave nodded and nervously adjusted the chin strap on his crash helmet.

"I just wanted to warn you," said Webb with a chuckle, "so that you wouldn't be surprised if they bounced a beer can off your crash helmet. Of course we could clear them off the rock shelf—"

"They can stay there as far as I'm concerned," said Dave determinedly. "I'm not going to let them bother me."

"That's the spirit." Webb reached into the cockpit and clapped Dave on the back. "Now fasten your safety belt, put on your goggles, go up there to the starting line and drive the way I've taught you. Good luck."

Negley Foxcroft's voice vibrated over the public address system, "Coming up to the starting line, Number 3, a Model A special, driven by Dave Neil of Milltown."

Me, said Dave to himself, That's my name being given to a crowd over a loudspeaker. Holy crow!

"Take a good look at this Model A, ladies and gentlemen," said Negley Foxcroft. "It's a homemade special. Just about a year ago it was scattered all over automobile graveyards. It took a lot of hard work and ingenuity to put those old discarded parts together in a good, safe, fast racing car. Yes sir. Dave and his Model A special represent millions of American boys who love to work on auto engines, make something out of nothing. The Sports Car Club is proud to welcome young drivers like Dave and their cars into this competition. We feel sure that Dave and other novice drivers like him will some day graduate into the ranks of senior competitors and drive their own specials in many of the hill climbs and road races we sponsor from coast to coast."

Dave's face was taut, red. Gosh what a build-up, he thought. Negley Foxcroft really lays it on with a trowel. Holy smoke, I'm practically a celebrity. A kid asks me for an autograph, the public address system introduces me to the crowd. I don't deserve it. It's Webb who should get all the credit. If it weren't for him I'd be just another twerp from the Milltown Hot Rod Club. I've got to repay Webb by showing those dopes up on the rock shelf at the S bend that—

"All set, lad?" It was Angus MacKenzie who was the official starter for the hill climb. Angus was all dressed up in a tweed jacket and a tweed cap woven in the tartan of the MacKenzie clan.

The sight of Angus eased a little of Dave's tension. He smiled nervously and said, "All set, Angus." His right hand automatically pulled the gear shift down into first, leaving a small stain of sweat on the plastic knob.

"Rrrelax lad," said Angus. "I'm going to give you a deliberrate 1-2-3 and then Go. O.K.?"

Dave swallowed, nodded his crash helmet; the chin strap suddenly felt very tight around his throat.

"All rrready?" Angus raised a green flag as his voice clicked off the seconds "deliberrately," "1-2-3," the green flag flashed. "*Go!*"

Arrooom. Dave almost peeled rubber—almost but not quite. Traction was not broken, seconds were not lost in screaming tires. The Model A's rear wheels turned fast but their tires did not lose their grip on the road; instead they sent the hot rod hurtling up the hill.

This was it, the big chance. And the Model A was ready. Never had its roar been so confident. It seemed to sense that the driver at its wheel now knew exactly what he was doing—how to handle the wheel, when to shift, when to pour on the power, when to brake.

An exultant voice spoke in Dave's ear. Listen to that wonderful engine. This is the payoff for all the hard work you put into it. Feel the wind rush by your

261

crash helmet, feel the powerful pull when your foot tromps the accelerator. You're going like a rocket but you're not foolishly challenging a constable. And you've got everything under control. Makes a big difference doesn't it? You bet it does.

Shift here. Don't double-clutch—it isn't necessary shifting up. Now tromp that accelerator. *Arroomm.* Listen to that engine. Shift—shift again to high now that you're over the first crest. Then step on it again. *Arroomm.* Race 'er right up to the cut-out point you selected on your practice run—Doc Brown's driveway. Now hit the brake; slow down for the S bend. Remember: the best driver is the one who wins at the slowest speed. Safety Fast. Stay out of those dangerous time-wasting spins.

Dave was in the first bend of the S turn cutting from the center of the road to the right, parallel and close to the rock shelf. Everything was under control. He wasn't spinning tail first into the stone fence with locked brakes. By braking at the cut-out point he had come into the curve at a maneuverable speed which had allowed him to cut sharply into the curve's apex. He was there now, shifting swiftly, smoothly, double clutching as he shifted down from third to second in the steep curve and then—pour on the coal!

Arroomm. He pushed the accelerator against the floor, asking for power, all of it. The Model A's engine roared its answer, obedient, brash, wonderful. Up the

262

hill toward the inside curve of the S bend hurtled the hot rod and its driver.

The climb was more gradual between the first and second bends and Dave shifted into high as he raced toward the second cut-out point, a tall hemlock stretching up from the ravine on the left. As he roared up to his cut-out point he hit his brakes, slowed down for the second curve, maneuvered nicely from right to left.

Ponk. He had reached the apex of the curve when his keen ears detected a sharp discordant noise. Something wrong with the engine? No. Its roar was as strong as ever as he double clutched, shifted down into second. A loose stone from the rock shelf then? No. A flash of anger swept over Dave as he identified the cause of the noise—a beer can, courtesy of those clucks in the hot rod club.

But it didn't bother him—he didn't let it. He had skillfully steered his Model A around the second bend of the S turn. Now he poured on the power. *Arroomm.* Away went the Model A up out of the S turn to the top of the hill. *Rur-ruh, rur-ruh, rur-ruh.* Higher, higher, higher revved the Model A's engine, reaching a pitch which told Dave's trained ears that it was time to shift to third.

Arrooomm. He had shifted swiftly, smoothly, then given his car the gun, sending the hot rod blasting along the ridge road bordered with a blur of spectators. Now no constable waited, bait in a speed trap. The perverted excitement of lawbreaking was missing but missing too were the fear and the pangs of a guilty conscience. Now the ride along the ridge past the cider mill and Lockwood's farm was an exhilarating rush, a thrilling climax to a painfully acquired privilege—a legal race against time in a greatly improved hot rod.

Suddenly the checkered flag flashed into Dave's line of vision—finish line! Dave's foot jerked off the accelerator, his hands loosened their grip on the wheel as he fanned his brakes and deftly guided his Model A to a stop. Then in the comparative quiet produced by the reduced speed he heard it and listened incredulously—it was applause and even some cheering. For whom? For Dave Neil, formerly of the Milltown Hot Rod Club.

Negley Foxcroft's voice came crashing through the public address system and Dave's fingers, trembling a little from the strain of the run, stopped fumbling with the crash helmet's chin strap: "Car No. 3, a Model A special driven by Dave Neil of Milltown, has just finished its run. Now here's the official time—and don't forget, folks, that this time is not for a flat straight stretch but for a long steep hill climb up through an S bend; the official time for car number three is one minute, twenty-nine and two-tenths seconds!"

One minute, twenty-nine and two-tenths seconds.

Dave silently repeated the time with a sudden warming rush of satisfaction. How much faster that was than the two minutes and seven seconds made that fateful night of the challenge against Constable Currie. Better than thirty seconds faster! It showed what a difference real mechanical and driving skill could make. Dave's fingers finished unfastening the chin strap as he gratefully compared not only his time for the run but the circumstances under which the run was made, one illegal and foolhardy, the other approved by the community and reasonably safe. A world of a difference. But Dave wasn't completely satisfied. The time for the hill climb, like the Model A's engine, was good but it could always be bettered. It might be bettered in the afternoon run by slightly improving either the engine or the driving performance.

Dave's thoughts were interrupted by Negley Foxcroft's rich voice marching out of the loudspeaker: "Coming up to the starting line now in a V-8 special is Max Werner of the Milltown Hot Rod Club. Like Dave Neil, his opponent in this novice class, Max has—"

Like me? Dave asked, frowning at what sounded like an insult, unintentional perhaps, but insulting just the same. Why Max is about as much like me, said Dave to himself, as Webb Walden is like Negley Foxcroft. For one thing, Max is not much of a mechanic.

He doesn't have any real love for automobile engines, he just uses them as another way of showing off. And that's the way he drives too, show-off stuff. Still—a shadow of a doubt shaded Dave's sharp criticism of his rival; it would be just like Max to rocket that V-8 up through the S bend and—

Eeeeeekk. A dozen trapped mice seemed to squeal through the loudspeaker. And Negley Foxcroft's rich voice frantically pursued the squeal, "Did Max give his V-8 the gun? He sure did. That, folks, is what hot rodders call peeling rubber. Max really peeled it— yes sir!"

Dave scowled. Negley Foxcroft was sometimes just a clown who didn't know what he was talking about. Didn't he realize that peeling rubber meant breaking traction and that breaking—

The loudspeaker rasped over the raucous sound of the V-8's engine, "Max is already up over that first rise, folks, and listen to that V-8 roar! He's out of sight now but in just a second we'll have a flash from signal station number 1 in the S bend."

Dave's scowl softened into a worried frown— "already up over the first rise"? Max got there pretty fast and from the solid sound of the V-8's engine he was—

"Report from signal station number 1," rasped Negley Foxcroft over the V-8's roar. "Max put his V-8 into a power slide and went around the first loop of the S bend on two wheels. This boy is really—"

Power slide? Dave's mouth dropped open, his eyes stared glassily at the loudspeaker hanging high over the finish line. Negley Foxcroft must be out of his mind. Max didn't know the difference between a power slide and a cut-out point. How could Max—

The loudspeaker again interrupted Dave's thoughts: "Listen to that hot rod roar, folks! Our mikes on the hill are picking up the noise of that powerful V-8 engine, and those cheers coming in now are from members of the Milltown Hot Rod Club watching from the second loop in the S bend. They sound pretty proud of their president. Yes sir!"

Dave's mouth snapped shut, his stare turned into a glare as he thought, Those same stupid hot rodders who threw that empty beer can at me are cheering Max. By gosh it isn't—

Clonk. Bonk-eeek. Strange sounds were spurting from the loudspeaker. The loud steady roar of the V-8 had suddenly deteriorated into a weird cacophony. And all at once Negley Foxcroft was talking like an announcer who has lost his sponsor: "Uh, something seems to have gone wrong, folks. Give us a flash, station 2. Come in station 2!"

Straightening up behind the wheel of the Model A, Dave automatically pulled on his goggles, pushed in his clutch pedal, reached for the magneto switch.

Something had happened to the V-8. Good. It served Max right, trouble was just what he deserved. No, that was the wrong way to look at it. Of course Max was a show-off driver but suppose he had gone into a spin, crashed into the stone fence, hurtled down into the ravine?

"Report from station 2!" rasped Negley Foxcroft and his rich voice was now grim, a newscaster bearing bad tidings, "Station 2 requests fire engine and emergency truck!" Negley Foxcroft's grim voice hurried on. "Fire engine and emergency truck, go to station 2 immediately. Fire engine and—"

Fire! A mental picture of disaster flashed before Dave's worried eyes as he started his engine, shifted into first: Max and his V-8 spinning into the stone fence, crashing down into the ravine; the V-8 bursting into flames with Max unconscious and trapped in the cockpit.

Arooom. The Model A rushed down the road with Dave grimly gripping the wheel. Max was stupid, Max was a show-off, but Max must be helped.

Racing back along the ridge between lines of staring spectators, Dave quickly reached the top of the hill. He took his foot off the accelerator, double-clutched, and shifted neatly down into second. Using his transmission as a brake but maintaining much of his speed, he roared down toward the second loop of the S turn, preparing himself for the tragic mess that might be there.

Then he saw it. He saw it as he slowed down, with the Model A backing off its pipes. And what he saw turned Dave's grimness into bewilderment. For what he had imagined as a tragic mess turned out to be something quite different.

Max Werner's V-8 was in trouble. But it hadn't crashed into the stone fence, hurtled into the ravine. It had banged into one of the big spike-shaped stones, stalled ignominiously, and was smoking. And Max, far from being pinned unconscious in the wreckage of his hot rod as it went up in smoke, was standing at a careful distance from his car spraying it with the fire extinguisher he had professed to despise.

Dave's grim fear for Max had faded before his bewilderment. Now it disappeared altogether as Dave realized what Max was doing—standing there in that ridiculous football helmet spraying chemicals on a steaming bathtub. For Dave could now see that it was steam—not smoke—and that the engine was either overheated or had blown a gasket. But Max in his panic had thought first of fire and, grabbing his extinguisher, had scrambled out of the cockpit and started spraying.

A crowd had gathered. The members of the Milltown Hot Rod Club had swarmed down off the rock shelf. And like Dave they had run the gamut of emotions: fear for their hero, then surprise and bewilderment, and finally derision and scornful humor at his panic-stricken performance. For it was obvious now to everyone except Max that it was steam, not smoke, that was pouring up from under the V-8's hood.

The scornful humor of the hot rod club increased as officials in white coveralls took charge and exposed the real reason for the engine's steamy failure, a blown head gasket, the same cause that had once stopped Dave's Model A.

"Hey Max, where's the fire?"

It was a taunt from hot rodder Billy Forney.

With his football helmet at a comical angle, his fire extinguisher dripping pathetically, Max turned on his tormentor. But he didn't snarl or swear as he would have in the past. He just stared with stricken eyes like a bull who has snorted and bellowed and thrown its weight around until at last it stands exhausted, humiliated, stripped of its power, and surrounded by a jeering crowd.

Arrooo. It wasn't an engine being revved up, it was the whine of the fire engine's siren. Its arrival increased Max's humiliation. No fire. The firemen were frustrated and took it out on Max with good-natured jibes: "What'sa matter, Max? Can't you tell the difference between steam and smoke?"

"There's a fine for false alarms, Max."

And from the fire chief, who was holding another

fire extinguisher, "Listen Max, don't blow your top just 'cause you blew a gasket. Save your fire extinguisher for the real thing. And now hand over the one you wasted and take this replacement."

"I don't need it," said Max sullenly.

"Course you need it," said the fire chief. "You can't make your afternoon run without a fire extinguisher— it's against the rules."

"I won't be makin' any afternoon run," said Max in a flat voice.

"Why not?" said the fire chief. "It only takes a couple of hours to put in a new head gasket."

"Not for me it don't," said Max, hanging his head in the red and gold football helmet. "I've never changed a head gasket. I wouldn't know how to start."

"Too bad," said the fire chief with a shrug of his shoulders. "Hey Charlie!" he yelled to the driver of the wrecking truck which had just arrived. "You gonna tow this leaky bathtub back down the hill?"

"Leaky bathtub." That was the final blow. Max reeled away under it and sat down on a rock by the side of the road. The fire engine roared off. The wrecking truck took the V-8 in tow and Negley Foxcroft's voice over the public address system said, "Well folks, in just a few minutes now the course will be clear and the hill climb will be resumed.

"And listen folks—here's a real hot item. Yes sir. We just got a report from station 2 on the accident to car

No. 5 driven by Max Werner." Negley Foxcroft's voice warmed to the occasion. He was in his element now. He had news for his audience and he was presenting it in what he thought was appropriate style, folksy, jocose. And where, in his ignorance, he had once poured too much enthusiasm on Max Werner, he now went off balance the other way and poked fun at his fallen hero.

"Well, folks, this is the story of the steaming bathtub. You remember what car No. 5 looked like—it looked sort of like a bathtub, it did indeed. Well, our old friend Max Werner went into a bit of a spin on the big bend near station 2 and when that bathtub of his struck the stone fence it sprang a leak—a very steamy leak. Yes sir. Ha-ha.

"Well, our old friend Max thought his car was on fire so he grabbed his fire extinguisher and let fly, yes sir! Now what really happened, folks, is that the V-8 blew a gasket and it was just like pulling the plug in the bathtub. Ha-ha.

"Well folks, I'm sure we're all glad Max didn't get hurt—except maybe his pride and we know Max is going to be a good sport about this setback. And if he can fix that leak in his bathtub—ha-ha—he'll—"

"Max."

The red and gold football helmet was leaning far over, resting on Max's arms which were supported by his knees.

"Hey, Max." Dave gently tapped the ridiculous helmet.

The helmet rose reluctantly and revealed the stricken face, "Wha'd *you* want?"

"Ride down the hill with me."

"What for?"

"Well, you want to replace that head gasket don't you—so you can make your second run this afternoon."

The helmet dropped and the voice, dropping with it, lost its sullenness and bogged down in despair, "You know darned well I've never replaced a head gasket."

Dave tapped the helmet. "Listen Max, I'll help you."

The helmet came up slowly, the face under it incredulous. "You crazy or something?"

Dave grinned. "Maybe. I got in a jam once, Max. I blew a gasket, too. Webb Walden helped me. It's not that I want to help you particularly, Max; it's just that I want to be like Webb Walden. Get it?"

"Maybe," said Max slowly.

"Well then, come on. Let's get down to the pits before they close the course again."

They rode down the hill together, with the Model A backing proudly off its pipes. Applause from the crowd along the course mixed with the popping sound of the hot rod's dual exhaust. Dave grinned and said generously, "That applause is for us, Max."

"It is like heck," said Max, "it's for you."

Dave glanced to his right. Was Max sore, envious? No. He just looked like a patient who had swallowed a pill and found it bitter. The football helmet was off now, the sideburns were visible and the long hair was blowing in the breeze. He looked pathetic. For the bluster and swagger were gone and in their place was just a deflated windbag, a pitiful character.

As the Model A rolled down to the stone bridge, Negley Foxcroft was still effervescing over the public address system: "Coming up to the starting line now folks, in his Ford-Duesenberg, is one of the finest drivers in the East, Webb Walden. Let's give him a great big hand."

While the applause still rattled over the loud-speakers, Negley Foxcroft rushed on, "Incidentally folks, Webb is now working on an all-Duesenberg racing car which will probably win top honors at the big hill climbs and road races sponsored by the Sports Car Club.

"Y'know, folks, it takes a whale of a lot of mechanical skill to rebuild one of those old Duesenbergs but our boy Webb Walden—"

Bang-bang-bang. The Model A, backing off its pipes, derisively backfired into Negley Foxcroft's bibble-babble. The crowd laughed. Dave chuckled and, glancing sideways, was glad to see a faint smile brighten the corners of Max's mouth.

The Model A was now almost abreast of the Ford-

Duesenberg and Dave saw Webb Walden sitting solemnly behind the wheel in his goggles and white crash helmet, ready but relaxed. There, thought Dave, is the real thing, a wonderful car, an expert driver.

Webb seemed to feel Dave's glance. He looked at the approaching Model A, caught Dave's eye, jerked his thumb in the direction of the loudspeaker, grinned, and shook his head. Braking to a stop beside the Ford-Duesenberg, Dave heard Webb's deep voice cut through the torrent of words pouring from the loudspeaker, "The *fourth* battle of Bull Run!"

Dave laughed. But wasn't Webb surprised to see Max Werner sharing the front seat of the Model A? Apparently not. Maybe Webb had known it would work out that way. His voice was again breaking through the loudspeaker's spiel, "Not a bad run you made, Dave. But you'll improve on it this afternoon."

Not a bad run? Yes, thought Dave, that was just about it. Not bad. But I can improve on it. And some day, by gosh, I'll be behind the wheel of Webb's Duesenberg and set a mark that will make the Sports Car Club sit up and take notice.

Webb was asking a question, "Does Max think he can get that head gasket fixed in time for the second run?"

"I'm going to help him," said Dave.

Webb didn't say anything but the white crash helmet nodded its approval as the Model A pulled over to the side of the road and the voice of starter Angus MacKenzie said, "All right, mon, I'll give you a deliberrate 1-2-3 and then Go. All set?"

"Check."

Angus MacKenzie raised the green flag and "deliberrately" ticked off the seconds, "1-2-3." The green flag flashed. *"Go!"*

Arrrooooooommmmmmmmm.

It was a wonderful, ear-splitting, soul-shattering sound that crackled over the public address system and echoed and re-echoed up the winding stone-shelved course.

Mouths open, eyes wide, Max and Dave watched the Ford-Duesenberg rocket up the hill into the S bend. There was no protesting squeal from tires that had peeled rubber; nor was there any sound of the shift into second, so swiftly and smoothly was it made. There was just that one great wonderful roar for the ears; and for the eyes one swift image flashing; and for the heart the unforgettable feeling of real friendship between men who understand engines and speed.